"You cannot fight mediocrity with
mediocrity from another angle."

—Jon Malli
Michigan Badlands

MATURE READERS!

SUPER COUPLE MISSING!

GEORGY PORGY STRIKES AGAIN.

ZOSIMOS

UGGNNNNN

RACHEL...

DID WE--

I-I WAS--

HAVING A N-NIGHTMARE.

A TERRIBLE NIGHTMARE.

OH, GOD IN HEAVEN.

PLEASE DON'T.

NO...

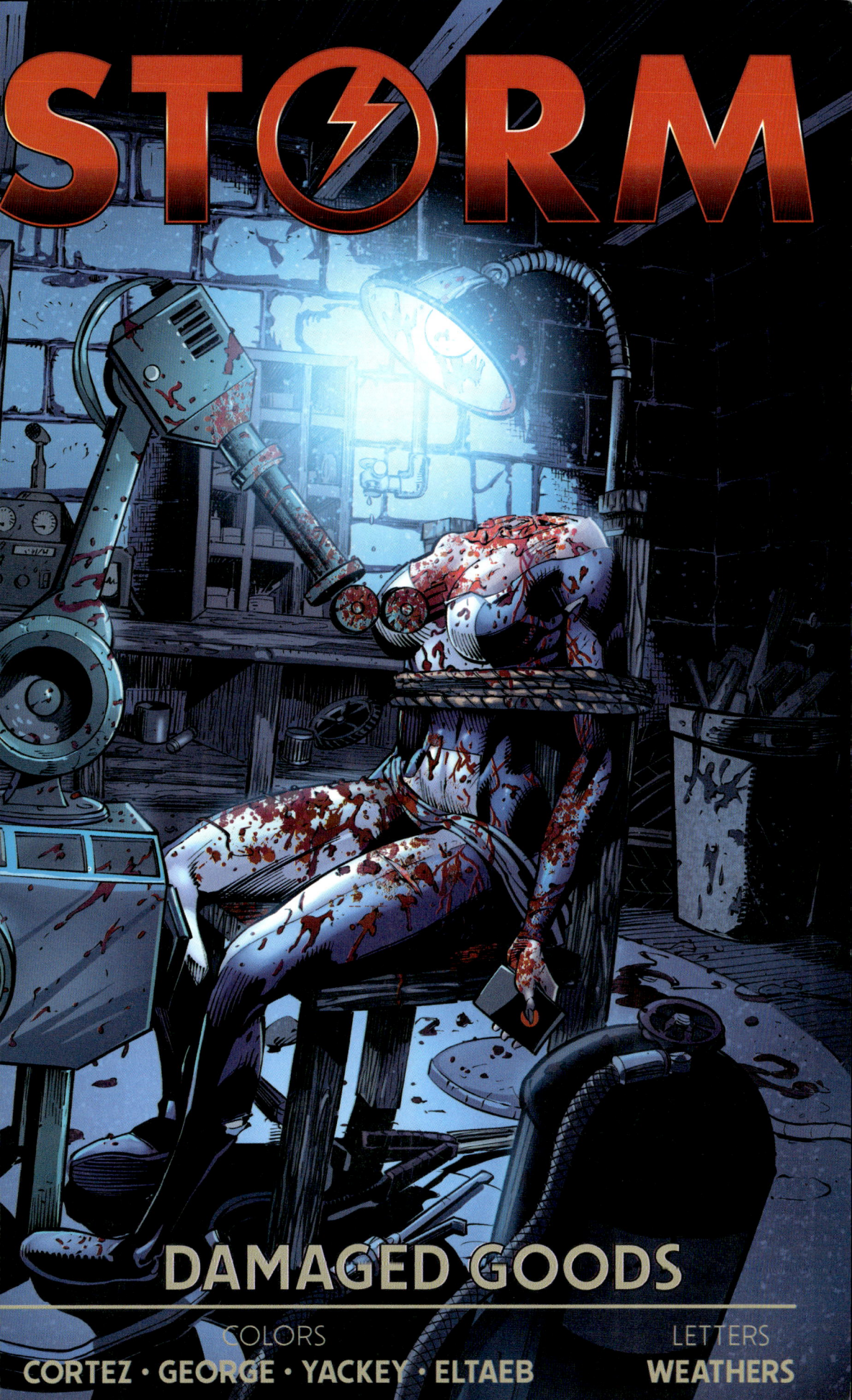

"IN TERROR
AND BLOOD.

"GOOD
EVENING--

IN A VICIOUS FOUR-WEEK KILLING SPREE,
MURDERING SIX OF EARTH'S MOST ELITE
SUPERHUMAN TASK FORCE, OMEGA STORM.
POLICE HAVE FOUND NO WITNESSES,
FINGERPRINTS, OR DNA FOR THIS GOD KILLER.

"HIS FIRST VICTIM, FORMER NIGHTWALKER PROTÉGÉ
AND TEEN SENSATION, **RED ROBINETTE**, SUFFERED
REPEATED BLUNT FORCE TRAUMA TO THE BACK OF
HIS HEAD, KILLING HIM. HIS REAL NAME, RICARDO
PHILLIPE GRAYSTONE. HE WAS ONLY NINETEEN
YEARS OLD AND THE YOUNGEST ACTIVE-DUTY
MEMBER OF OMEGA STORM.

"THE WORLD WAS HORRIFIED A WEEK LATER,
WHEN A VIDEO WAS POSTED TO THE DARK WEB.
THE AUDIO, CONSISTING ONLY OF THE CHILDREN'S
NURSERY RHYME 'GEORGY PORGY, PUDDING PIE'
REPEATING ON A LOOP, SHOWING A MAN RAPING
AND MURDERING RED ROBINETTE.

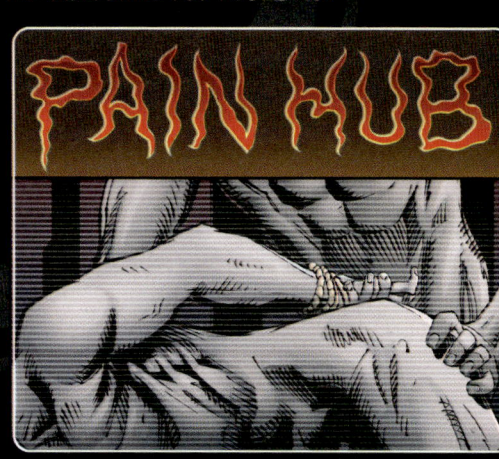

"NOW OVER ONE BILLION VIEWS AND COUNTING,
THE VIDEO WAS CAREFULLY EDITED, PRESUMABLY
BY THE KILLER, NOT TO REVEAL HIS IDENTITY. IT
SHOWS US ONLY THAT HE IS A HIGHLY AGGRESSIVE
WHITE MALE. JUDGING FROM HIS VICTIMS, HE
LIKELY HAS ABOVE-HUMAN STRENGTH AND/OR
OTHER ABILITIES.

"NEXT TO DIE WAS OPEN HOMOSEXUAL, **SIGIL**,
GUARDIAN OF THE GATES OF LIMBO AND LEADER OF
ITS ARMIES. CHOKED TO DEATH WITH HIS OWN
AMPUTATED PENIS, FORCED INTO HIS THROAT. HIS
CORRIDORS, NOW FOREVER SEALED. THE VIOLENT
SEXUAL NATURE OF THESE CRIMES, THE DESIRE TO
HUMILIATE OUR ICONS, HAS TURNED THE STOMACHS
OF EVEN THE MOST VETERAN INVESTIGATORS."

"THREE DAYS LATER, THE BRAZILIAN BOMBSHELL KNOWN AS *SIDEWINDER* WAS FORCED TO WATCH HER TWO DAUGHTERS, AGES EIGHT AND SIX, BE FED ALIVE TO AN ANACONDA. SEDATED RATS WERE THEN STITCHED INTO HER VAGINA, NEXT TO HER UNBORN CHILD. THE CHILD AND MOTHER BOTH DIED AS THE RATS WOKE, GNAWING THEIR WAY OUT.

LIVE 7 — Chloe Kunnel
Where is Georgy Porgy?
ords in Asia.   Man has relations with jellyfish. Claims sex life has never been better.

"IN JUST FOUR WEEKS, SIX HEROES HAD FALLEN PREY TO GEORGY PORGY'S BLOOD-SOAKED REIGN OF TERROR. RED ROBINETTE, SIDEWINDER, SIEGE, SIGIL, MAELSTROM, AND RACHEL ROGERS. HEROES. ROLE MODELS. TAKEN FROM US, DEFILED, AND KILLED IN HORRIFIC FASHION. AND NOW, SILENCE. BUT WHY?

"THE OMEGA STORM INITIATIVE WAS ENVISIONED THREE YEARS AGO BY U.S. PRESIDENT SEWARD, WHO, IN CONJUNCTION WITH THE U.N., VOWED TO CREATE A DETERRENT FOR ALL SUPERHUMAN, OR 'OMEGA' LEVEL THREATS. AFTER THE BATTLE OF NEW YORK SHOCKED THE WORLD, LEAVING U.S. PRESIDENT VAN HELSING DEAD--

LIVE 7 — Chloe Kunnel
Omega Storm Initiative.
The New Freedom Alliance promises to end offensive speech and defend free speech

"GEORGY PORGY'S LAST VICTIM, RACHEL ROGERS. BELOVED MATRIARCH, FOUNDING MEMBER OF OMEGA STORM AND WIFE OF TEAM LEADER RICK ROGERS. DETAILS OF HER DEATH ARE STILL UNDER LOCK AND KEY. RUMORS SAY SHE WAS DECAPITATED, AND HER HEAD IS STILL MISSING TO THIS DAY. OF COURSE, WE HERE AT CHANNEL 7 ONLY REPORT THE FACTS.

LIVE 7 — Chloe Kunnel
Omega Storm Initiative.
en better. Graveyard Shift returns from an unknown mission in Antarctica. Monolith in

"PERHAPS THE BIGGEST QUESTION HAS BEEN, WHERE IS OMEGA STORM'S RESPONSE? SIX MEMBERS HAVE BEEN MURDERED. WHY HAVEN'T THEY BROUGHT GEORGY PORGY TO JUSTICE? CONFIDENTIAL INFORMANTS SAY TEAM MORALE IS AT AN ALL-TIME LOW, WITH INFIGHTING GROWING SINCE TEAM LEADER RICK ROGERS' ABSENCE.

LIVE 7 — Chloe Kunnel
Omega Storm Initiative.
Government missing trillions in taxpayer dollars? Nothing to worry about says offi

"--AND THE U.N. SECRETARIAT BUILDING IN RUBBLE, WORLD GOVERNMENTS SWORE 'NEVER AGAIN,' REBUILDING AND COMBINING THEIR FORCES. OMEGA STORM WAS BORN. THREE YEARS LATER, OMEGA STORM HAS BEEN NO STRANGER TO CASUALTIES, LOSING SEVERAL MEMBERS IN MAJOR BATTLES ALREADY. THE MOST RECENT ROSTER INCLUDED--"

"REYKJAVIK'S #1 DAUGHTER, ACTRESS, AND SUPERMODEL, SALKA THORSDOTTIR, MAY BE FROM THE LAND OF FIRE AND ICE, BUT SHE'S BEEN PURE HEAT IN AMERICA, BURNING UP THE MEDIA MACHINE.

"AFTER BREAKING OFF HER RECENT FLING WITH ACTION STAR, JACK STONE, THIS TELEPATH AND SERIAL DATER IS BACK ON THE MARKET.

"THE 'INDESTRUCTIBLE MAN,' RICK 'VANGUARDIAN' ROGERS AND HIS BELOVED WIFE, RACHEL 'GHOST GIRL' ROGERS, THE VERY HEART OF OMEGA STORM.

ROG
CENTER FOR

"FORMER KSK OFFICER, PSION.

"CURRENTLY SERVING AS ACTING TEAM LEADER AND THE OLDEST OMEGA STORM MEMBER AT 42 YEARS OLD.

"ABLE TO FORGE PSIONIC WEAPONS AND MOVE OBJECTS WITH HIS MIND. HE CONTINUES TO INSPIRE AROUND THE GLOBE.

"CALIFORNIA'S THREE-TIME SURFING CHAMPION, JORDIE HAMILTON.

"WHEN HE FELL INTO HIS FATHER'S DARK MATTER EXPERIMENT, HE WAS TURNED INTO THE JUGGERNAUT KNOWN AS CRONOS.

"CANADA'S OWN, CHRISTIAN 'ARC' THOMAS.

"SIX WEEKS AFTER BEING STRUCK BY A PARTICLE BEAM AND LEFT COMATOSE, CHRISTIAN AWOKE WITH THE ABILITY TO CREATE BIOELECTRIC BLASTS.

...OUNDING OUT, THE TEAM ARE JUNIOR EMBERS, HI-FI AND TRACER. CIVILIAN NAMES ND POWERS ARE PROTECTED INFORMATION. EMOGRAPHICS SHOW MASSIVE INTEREST IN HIS PAIR FROM GIRLS AGED EIGHT TO WENTY-EIGHT. ANOTHER SUCCESS FOR OMEGA TORM--

...WHO, FOR TWO AND A HALF YEARS NOW, EVERY DAY, HAS BEEN ACTIVELY KEEPING US SAFE, MAKING US PROUD, STOPPING SUPER CRIMINALS IN THEIR TRACKS, AND FILLING UP THE OMEGA BLOCK AT MISKATONIC PRISON.

LIVE 7 — Chloe Kunnel — **Omega Storm Initiative.**
Adult film stars, Mia Cox Long and Dick Erector, double team congress and call for eco

VITH MERCHANDISING SALES ESTIMATED TO BE ITO THE BILLIONS, LEGIONS OF FANS AND ATERS SWARM SOCIAL MEDIA EVERY DAY JUST TO ET A GLIMPSE OF THEIR NEXT PRODUCT. MANY ILL REMEMBER LAST YEAR'S 'TICKLE ME, CRONOS' AS A SMASH CHRISTMAS HIT WITH NOT JUST KIDS UT ALSO COLLEGE GIRLS AND COLLECTORS.

"BUT, WITH ALL THEIR SUCCESS, THIS BLINDING FAILURE TO IDENTIFY AND STOP GEORGY PORGY SEEMS TO HAVE HURLED THIS TEAM OUT OF FOCUS. THE LOSS OF SIX TEAM MEMBERS IN FOUR WEEKS WAS THE SINGLE GREATEST LOSS OMEGA STORM HAS EVER SEEN.

LIVE 7 — Chloe Kunnel — **Omega Storm Initiative.**
economic reform.   Prisoners offended that they are locked up while others are free.

LIVE 7 — Chloe Kunnel — **Omega Storm Initiative.**
up while others are free.   New evidence for Flat Earth discovered. Also, flat moon?

IONE CUTTING THE GLOBAL PSYCHE SO MUCH AS HE DESTRUCTION OF THE ALL-AMERICAN ROGERS AMILY, A LOVING WIFE TO AN ADORING HUSBAND. IT EEMED, FOR A TIME, THAT NOTHING COULD EVER EPARATE THEM, THAT SOMEHOW THEY'D ALWAYS E THERE FOR EACH OTHER--AND US."

"RACHEL WOULD NOT WANT THE LEGACY THEY BUILT FOR OMEGA STORM TO JUST END IN A WHIMPER. SHE WOULD WANT HER TEAM TO UNITE AND RALLY ONCE MORE, AGAINST ALL THREATS. BUT THIS--THIS THUG, THIS MONSTER CALLED GEORGY PORGY, MUST BE STOPPED."

LIVE 7 — Chloe Kunnel — **Omega Storm Initiative.**
vered. Also, flat moon?   Armed teachers say students are literal Demons from Hell.

LIVE 7 — Chloe Kunnel — **Omega Storm Initiative.**
m Hell.   worms! it's what's for dinner. w.h.o. officials agree that worms are a nutritio

STOP!

OR WHAT, ARC? YOU GONNA *ZAP* ME?

≈HUFF≈ ≈HUFF≈ STAY ≈HUFF≈ *AWAY* FROM HER!

BRUH, *SALKA'S* ALL OVER ME IN THERE. SHE'S FINE AS HELL, AND YOU WANT ME TO MAKE ROOM FOR YOU AND HER?!

BESIDES, SHE DUMPED YOU LIKE EIGHT MONTHS AGO WHEN YOU DISAPPEARED ON THAT PRISON PLANET! SHE'S BEEN OPEN FOR BUSINESS EVER SINCE!

I'LL WIN HER BACK, DUDE!

YOU'RE BREAKING BRO CODE, 'NOS!

SHIT...

OK, FINE. LOOK, EVERYTHING'S COOL.

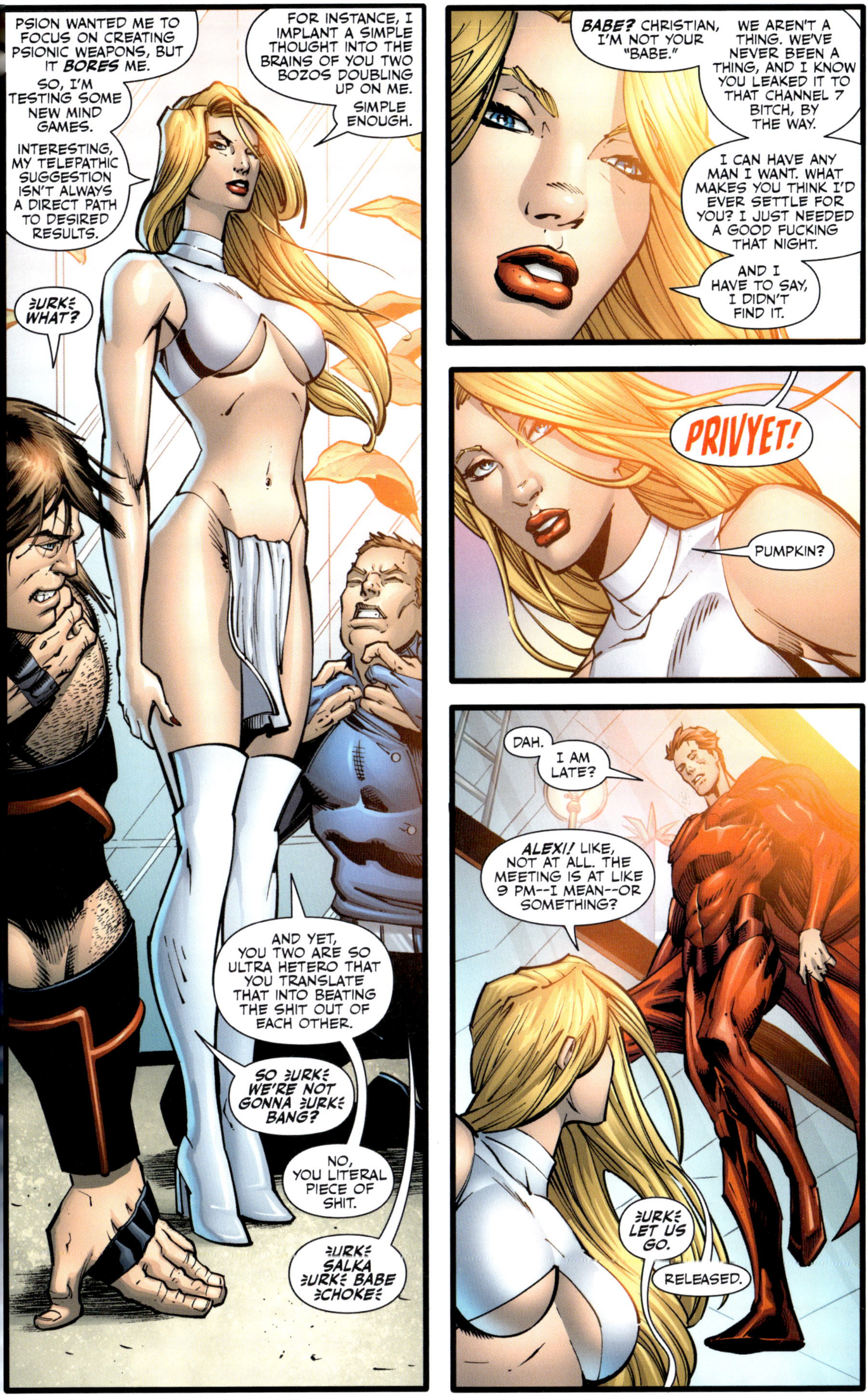

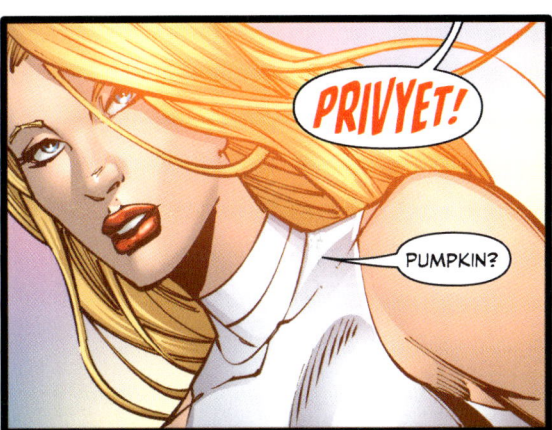

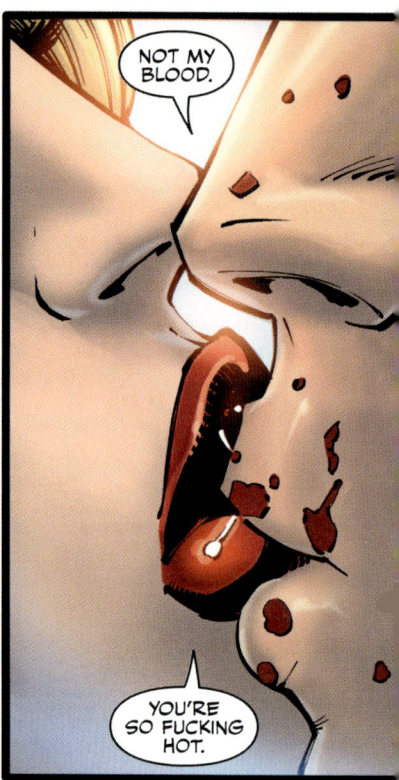

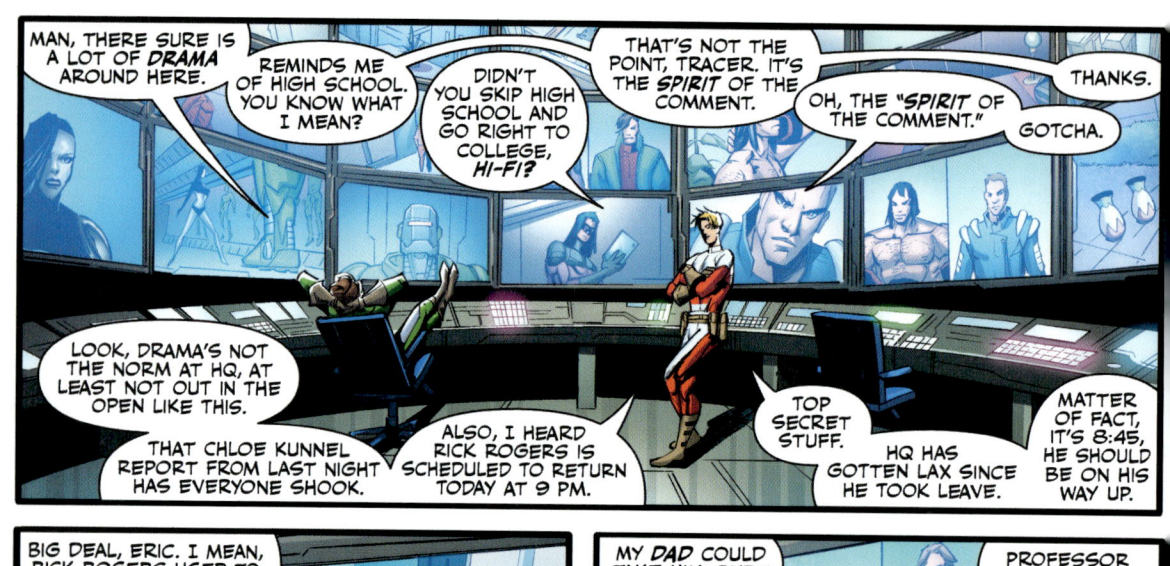

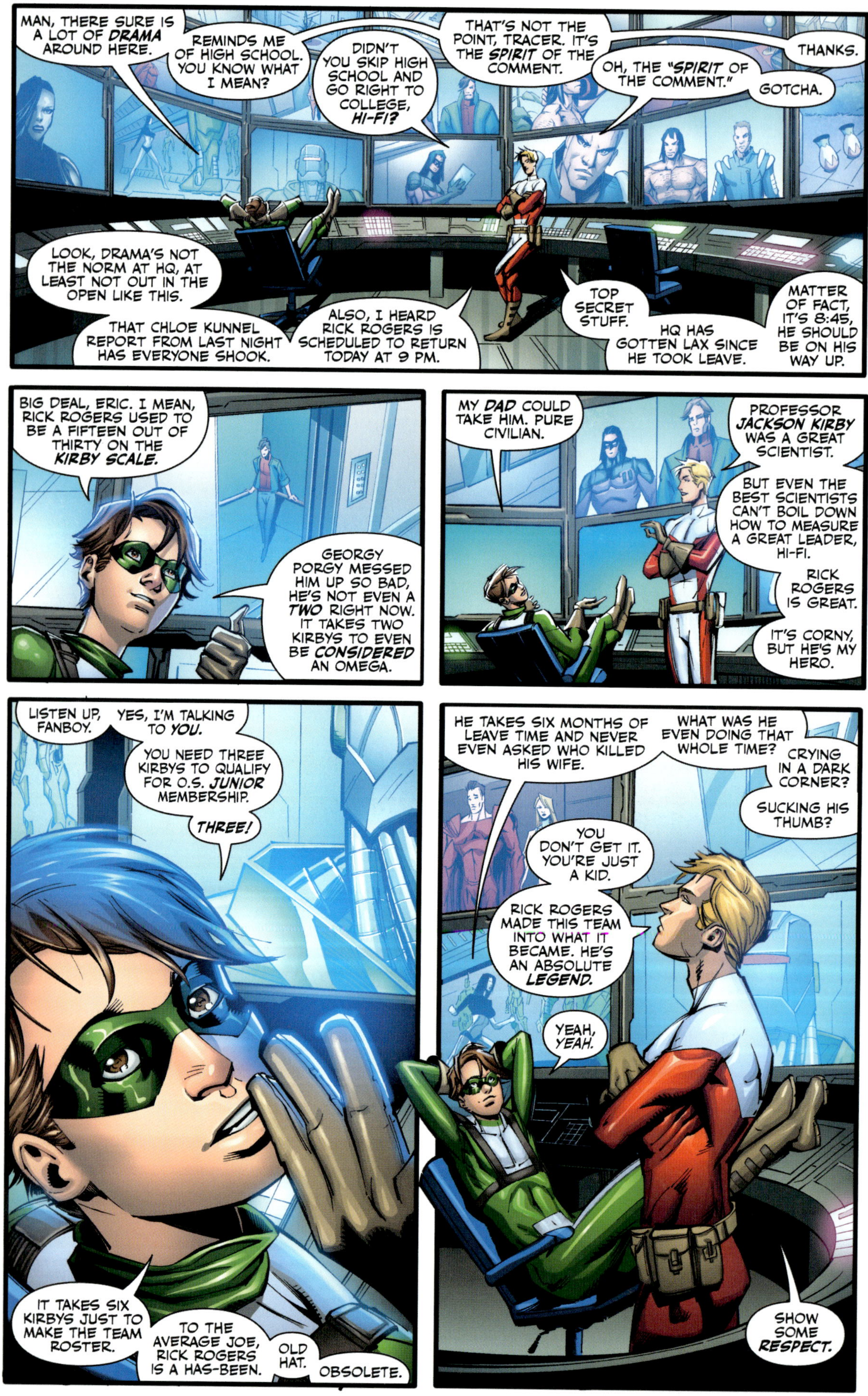

MAN, THERE SURE IS A LOT OF *DRAMA* AROUND HERE.

REMINDS ME OF HIGH SCHOOL. YOU KNOW WHAT I MEAN?

DIDN'T YOU SKIP HIGH SCHOOL AND GO RIGHT TO COLLEGE, *HI-FI?*

THAT'S NOT THE POINT, TRACER. IT'S THE *SPIRIT* OF THE COMMENT.

OH, THE "*SPIRIT* OF THE COMMENT."

GOTCHA.

THANKS.

LOOK, DRAMA'S NOT THE NORM AT HQ, AT LEAST NOT OUT IN THE OPEN LIKE THIS.

THAT CHLOE KUNNEL REPORT FROM LAST NIGHT HAS EVERYONE SHOOK.

ALSO, I HEARD RICK ROGERS IS SCHEDULED TO RETURN TODAY AT 9 PM.

TOP SECRET STUFF.

HQ HAS GOTTEN LAX SINCE HE TOOK LEAVE.

MATTER OF FACT, IT'S 8:45, HE SHOULD BE ON HIS WAY UP.

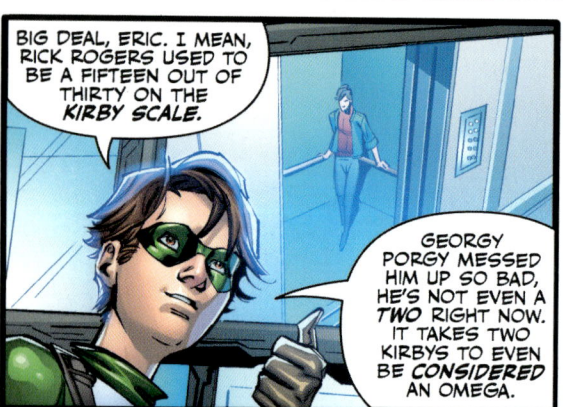

BIG DEAL, ERIC. I MEAN, RICK ROGERS USED TO BE A FIFTEEN OUT OF THIRTY ON THE *KIRBY SCALE.*

GEORGY PORGY MESSED HIM UP SO BAD, HE'S NOT EVEN A *TWO* RIGHT NOW. IT TAKES TWO KIRBYS TO EVEN BE *CONSIDERED* AN OMEGA.

MY *DAD* COULD TAKE HIM. PURE CIVILIAN.

PROFESSOR *JACKSON KIRBY* WAS A GREAT SCIENTIST.

BUT EVEN THE BEST SCIENTISTS CAN'T BOIL DOWN HOW TO MEASURE A GREAT LEADER, HI-FI.

RICK ROGERS IS GREAT.

IT'S CORNY, BUT HE'S MY HERO.

LISTEN UP, FANBOY.

YES, I'M TALKING TO *YOU.*

YOU NEED THREE KIRBYS TO QUALIFY FOR O.S. *JUNIOR* MEMBERSHIP.

THREE!

IT TAKES SIX KIRBYS JUST TO MAKE THE TEAM ROSTER.

TO THE AVERAGE JOE, RICK ROGERS IS A HAS-BEEN.

OLD HAT.

OBSOLETE.

HE TAKES SIX MONTHS OF LEAVE TIME AND NEVER EVEN ASKED WHO KILLED HIS WIFE.

WHAT WAS HE EVEN DOING THAT WHOLE TIME?

CRYING IN A DARK CORNER?

SUCKING HIS THUMB?

YOU DON'T GET IT. YOU'RE JUST A KID.

RICK ROGERS MADE THIS TEAM INTO WHAT IT BECAME. HE'S AN ABSOLUTE *LEGEND.*

YEAH, YEAH.

SHOW SOME *RESPECT.*

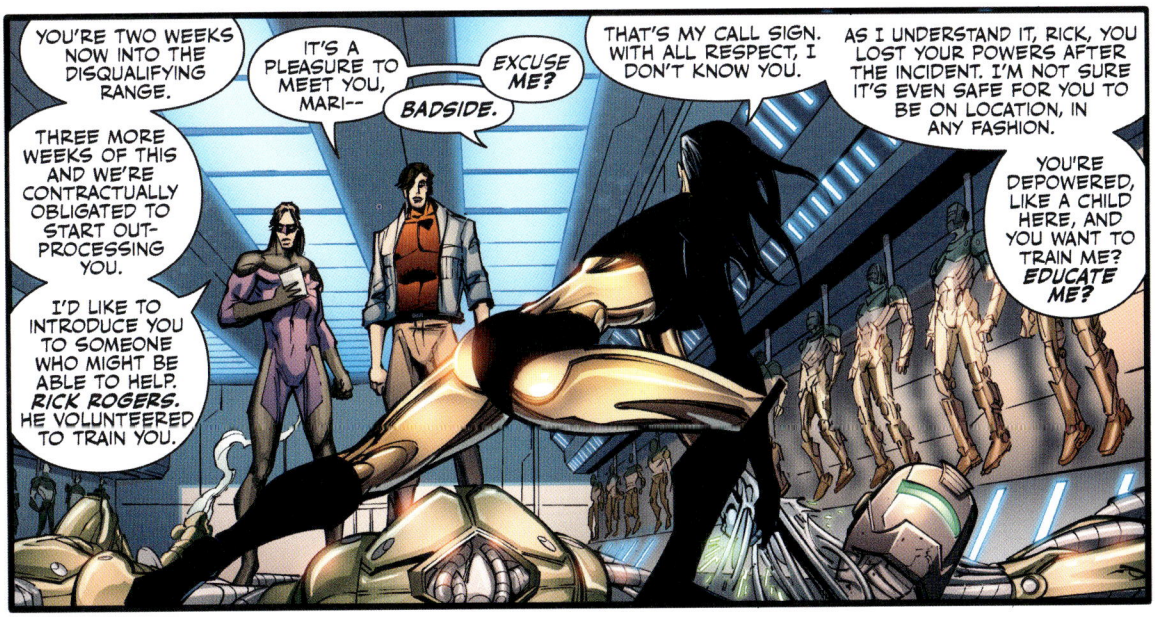

STOP PROGRAM.

UNFORTUNATELY, THINGS ARE NOT GOING IN THE DIRECTION WE HAD HOPED, MARIA.

YOU'RE TWO WEEKS NOW INTO THE DISQUALIFYING RANGE.

THREE MORE WEEKS OF THIS AND WE'RE CONTRACTUALLY OBLIGATED TO START OUT-PROCESSING YOU.

I'D LIKE TO INTRODUCE YOU TO SOMEONE WHO MIGHT BE ABLE TO HELP. RICK ROGERS. HE VOLUNTEERED TO TRAIN YOU.

IT'S A PLEASURE TO MEET YOU, MARI--

BADSIDE.

EXCUSE ME?

THAT'S MY CALL SIGN. WITH ALL RESPECT, I DON'T KNOW YOU.

AS I UNDERSTAND IT, RICK, YOU LOST YOUR POWERS AFTER THE INCIDENT. I'M NOT SURE IT'S EVEN SAFE FOR YOU TO BE ON LOCATION, IN ANY FASHION.

YOU'RE DEPOWERED, LIKE A CHILD HERE, AND YOU WANT TO TRAIN ME? EDUCATE ME?

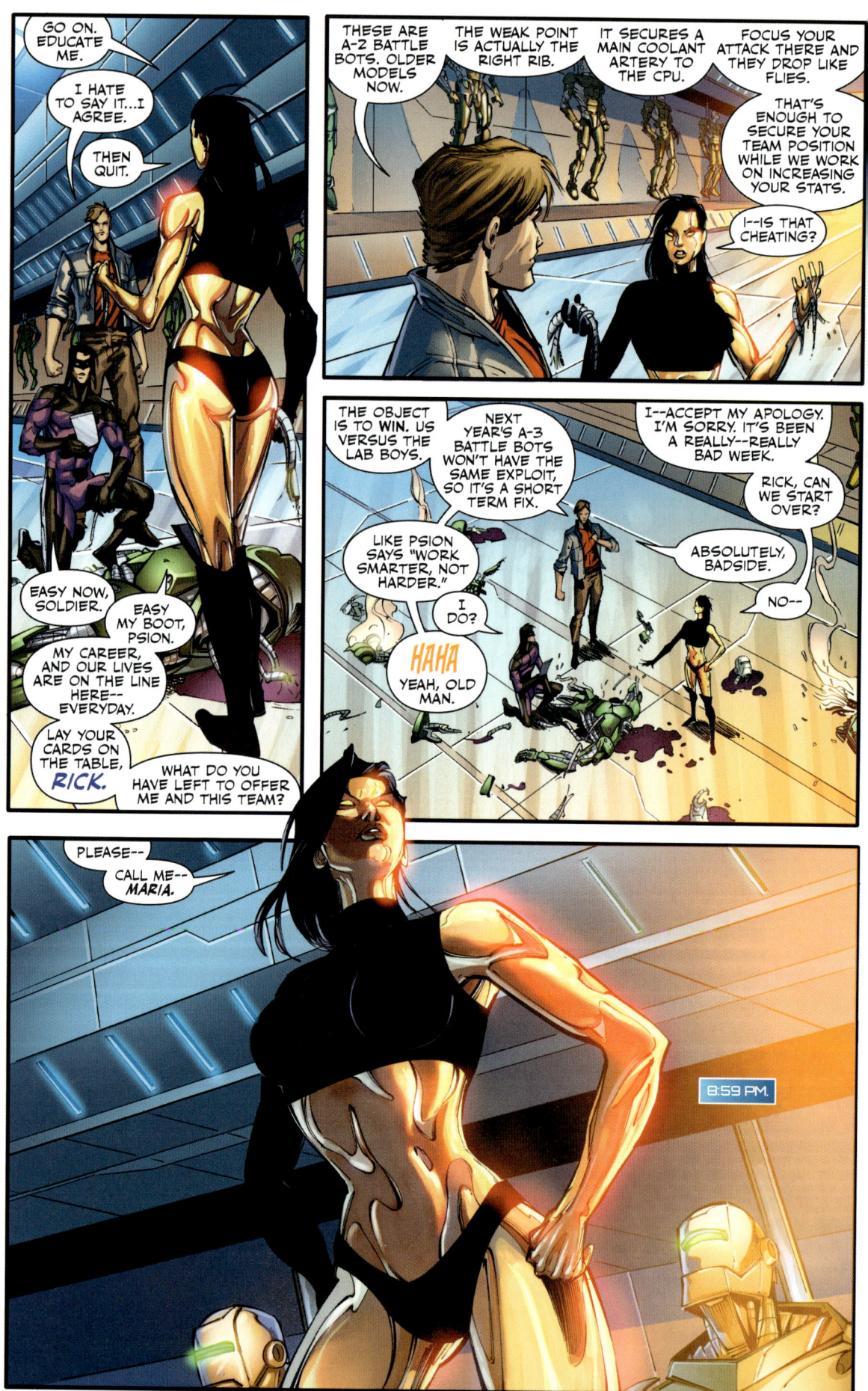

HMM, THAT'S ODD.

IT'S 9 PM, AIKO AND HIKARI ARE NOT IN THE BUILDING.

IT'S NOT UNUSUAL FOR HIKARI TO BE LATE, BUT AIKO IS *NEVER* LATE.

I'M NOT SEEING ANY UPDATES.

I'LL HAVE HI-FI AND TRACER TRY TO GET IN CONTACT WITH--

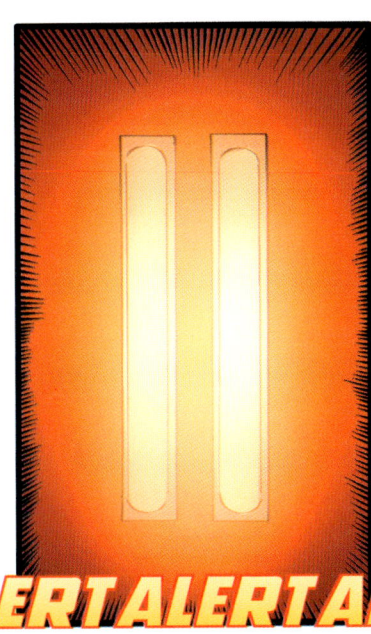

ALERT ALERT ALERT AL

ERT ALERT ALERT

THAT'S THE NEW LEVEL 1 ALARM, RICK.

THAT'S BAD.

WELCOME BACK, RICK! YOU MISS US?

ALWAYS! GOOD TO SEE YOU, PAL.

FORGIVE ME, BUT LEVEL 1? HOW BAD IS THAT?

WAR.

I HOPE IT'S NOT SPACE NAZIS AGAIN.

I HOPE YOU DON'T *CRY* AGAIN.

I'M SENSITIVE.

ALERT ALERT ALER

RTALER

TO THE *WAR ROOM!*

READY TO KILL.

READY TO SAVE!

BAH. GO SAVE TREE. LET *MEN* HANDLE.

WE GET IT. "ALERT, ALERT, ALERT."

WELL, I GUESS WE'RE GONNA BE STUCK IN HERE SMELLING EACH OTHER'S FARTS AGAIN.

OH, MAN.

THIS IS BAD. IT'S ALL OVER THE NET...

RICK, YOU GOTTA BE EXCITED!

WHEN YOU'RE ALL HOME SAFE, JORDIE, I WILL BE.

ERT ALERTALER TALERT ALERT ALE

THE HALL OF HONOR

A.K.A. THE WAR ROOM.

LET'S ALL GATHER 'ROUND.

DATA IS LOADING, WE'LL BE SET IN JUST A MINUTE.

RACHEL?

inator   December Man   Paramour

Ghost Girl   Vanguardian   Shado

WHY AM I UP THERE WITH THEM? THEY GAVE EVERYTHING, WHEN I NEVER DID.

RACHEL-- I'M SO SORRY, I COULDN'T-- I--

COWARD.

ATTENTION!

HIKARI MIFUNE WAS FOUND DEAD AN HOUR AGO.

REPORTS SAY SHE "EXPLODED FROM THE INSIDE."

HER SISTER, AIKO, IS MISSING.

NO.

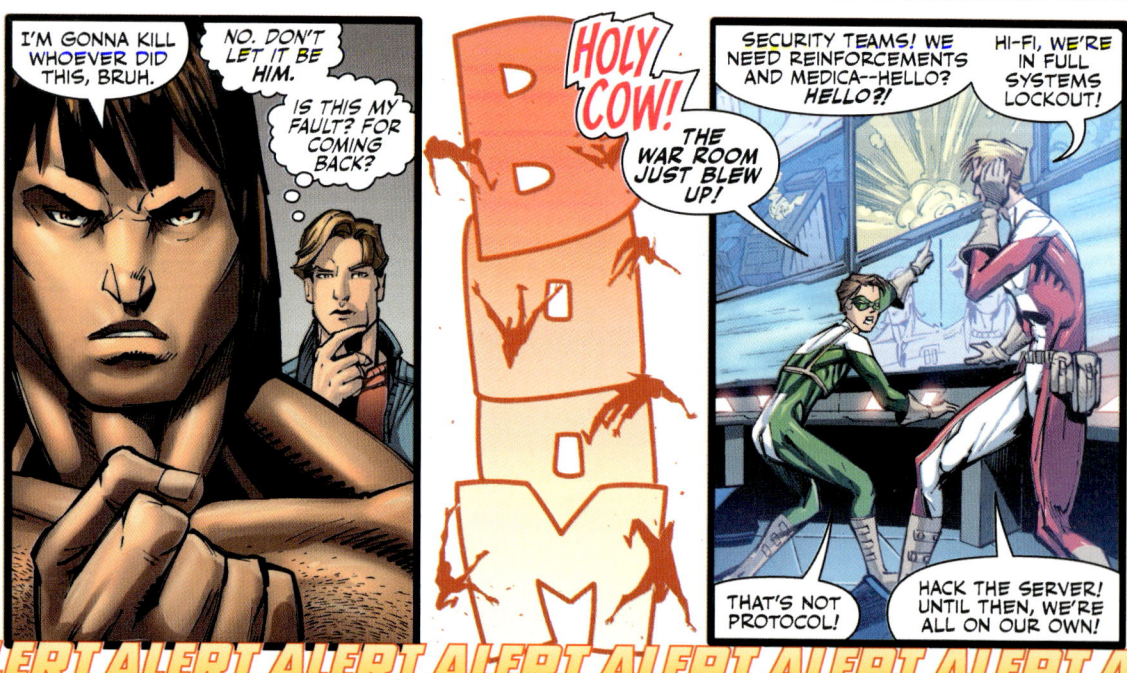

I'M GONNA KILL WHOEVER DID THIS, BRUH.

NO. DON'T LET IT BE HIM.

IS THIS MY FAULT? FOR COMING BACK?

HOLY COW!

BOOM

THE WAR ROOM JUST BLEW UP!

SECURITY TEAMS! WE NEED REINFORCEMENTS AND MEDICA--HELLO? HELLO?!

HI-FI, WE'RE IN FULL SYSTEMS LOCKOUT!

THAT'S NOT PROTOCOL!

HACK THE SERVER! UNTIL THEN, WE'RE ALL ON OUR OWN!

ALERT ALERT ALERT ALERT ALERT ALERT ALERT A

9:15 PM.

≡COUGH COUGH COUGH≡

≡COUGH COUGH≡

≡COUGH COUGH≡

≡COUGH≡

PSION? RED DAWN? CRONOS? SALKA?

IS ANYONE OUT THERE?

≡COUGH COUGH≡

I'M HERE!

ARC, ARE YOU OKAY?

MY LEG IS KILLING ME. MIGHT BE A MINOR BREAK, BUT I'M COOL...

HOLY SHIT, DUDE.

BRUH... WHAT WAS THAT?

THAT-- WAS FIRST STRIKE.

GET UP. GET READY.

WE'RE IN FOR--

COMPANY.

CLLAAAANNNNGGGG

OWW! DAING, BRUH!

THAT'S JUST A *TASTE!* I WANT ALL OF Y'ALL TO SUFFER!

WAR WASP IS IT?

YOU WANNA GET SOME OF THIS, CREEP?

--GET IN LINE!

GAHHHH!

TRYIN' TO POWER ON ME, B?

I BE THE O.G. OF BIO-ELECTRICITY.

NOT--RAP-- UHNNNNNNNNNN

I CAN'T GET INTO THEIR MINDS.

SOME KIND OF SHIELDING!

GETOFF MEBEFORE IRIPYOU INHALF!

I'M GONNA PUT YOU DOWN LIKE *OLD YELLER,* ARC!

I LOVED-- THAT-- DOG.

LITTLE HELP? ANYBODY! OOF!

WHAT'S THIS? I-I'M SCARED STIFF.

IT'S EASY TO BE BRAVE WHEN NEARLY INDESTRUCTIBLE. POWERFUL.

BUT TO BE LIKE THEM. VULNERABLE. POWERLESS.

COME HERE YOU LITTLE TWA-- AAAGGGHHH!

RED DAWN! CATCH!

SPASIBA.

BRING SOME OF THAT OVER HERE, BADSIDE! SEE WHAT HAPPENS.

WHAP

UGH!

I GOT ENOUGH FOR ALL OF Y'ALL!

YOU'RE ALL DEAD! AIN'T NOTHING GONNA CHANGE THAT!

WANNA BET?!

YEAH, I'LL TAKE THAT BET! SLOW ASS BITCH!

BADSIDE!

DAMN.

THAT'S IT RICK, ON YOUR FEET. MAKE DECISIONS. MAKE MOVES.

REMEMBER YOUR TRAINING.

"THE FEAR OF FAILURE--

"--MUST NEVER OUTWEIGH THE FEAR OF SUCCESS.

"YOU'VE PREACHED IT.

"NOW BELIEVE IT.

"PUT IT ALL ON THE LINE, RICK.

"LIKE THOSE BEFORE YOU.

"LIKE SHE DID.

RACHEL--

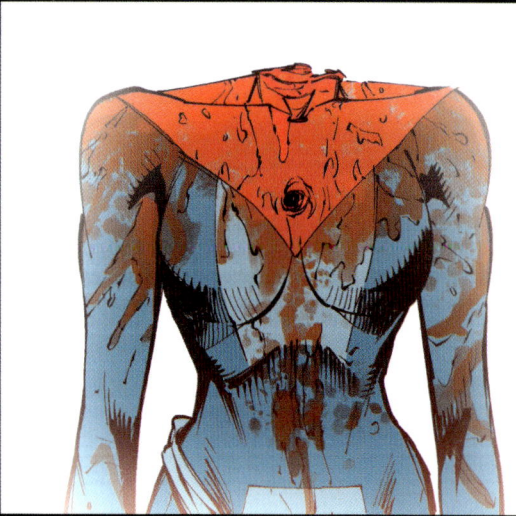

"LIKE--

"--ALL--

"--REAL--

"--HEROES--

"--DO."

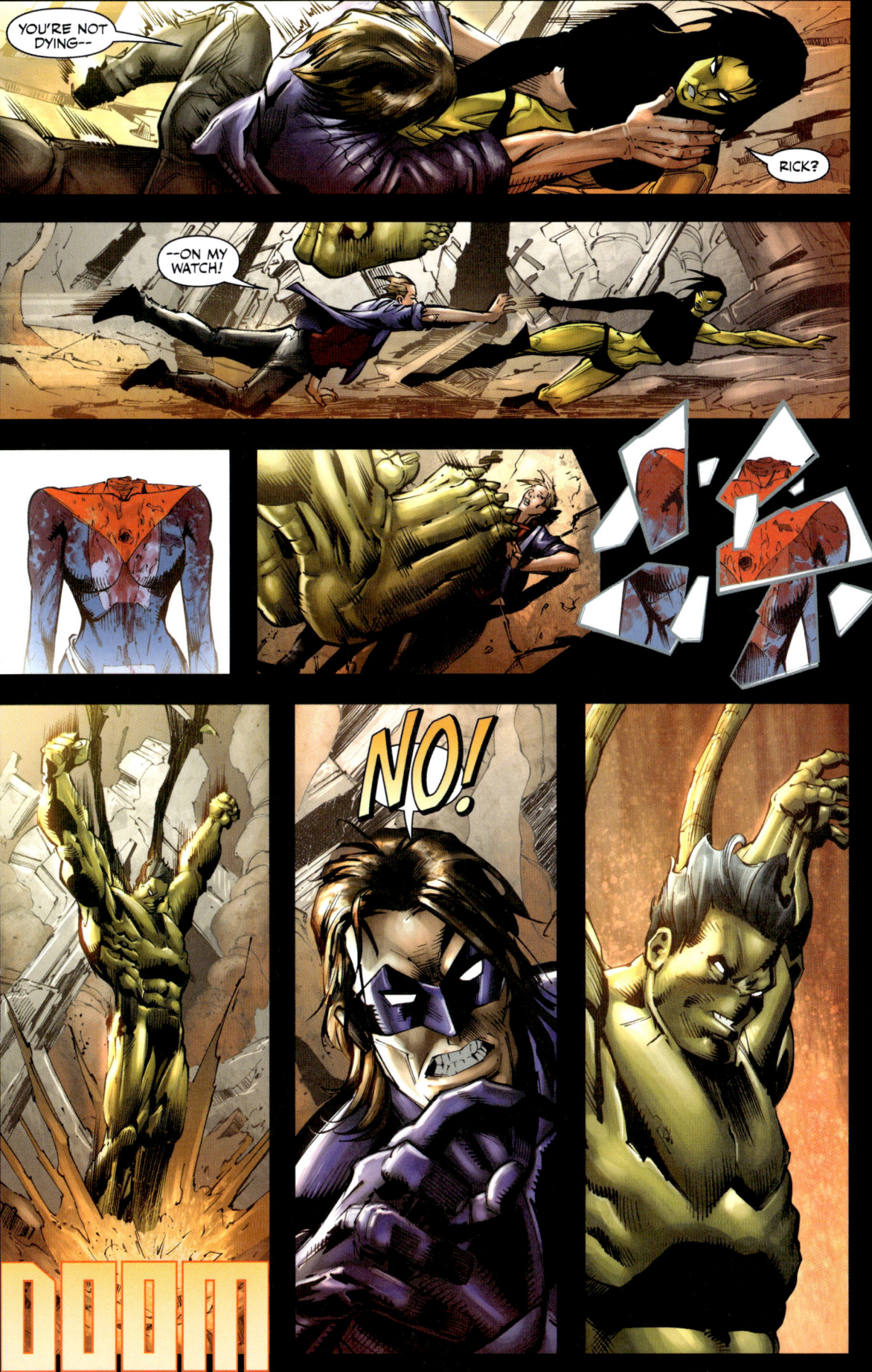

THIS IS POSSIBLE?

WAIT--

--STAAAAHHPP!

SO MUCH POWER. IN ONE MAN.

OH WOW, DUDE! HE COULDN'T DO ENERGY BLASTS BEFORE!

HE MUST BE PUSHING TWENTY FREAKING KIRBYS!

THIS IS INTENSE!

THE SHOCK WAVE ALONE! WHOA!

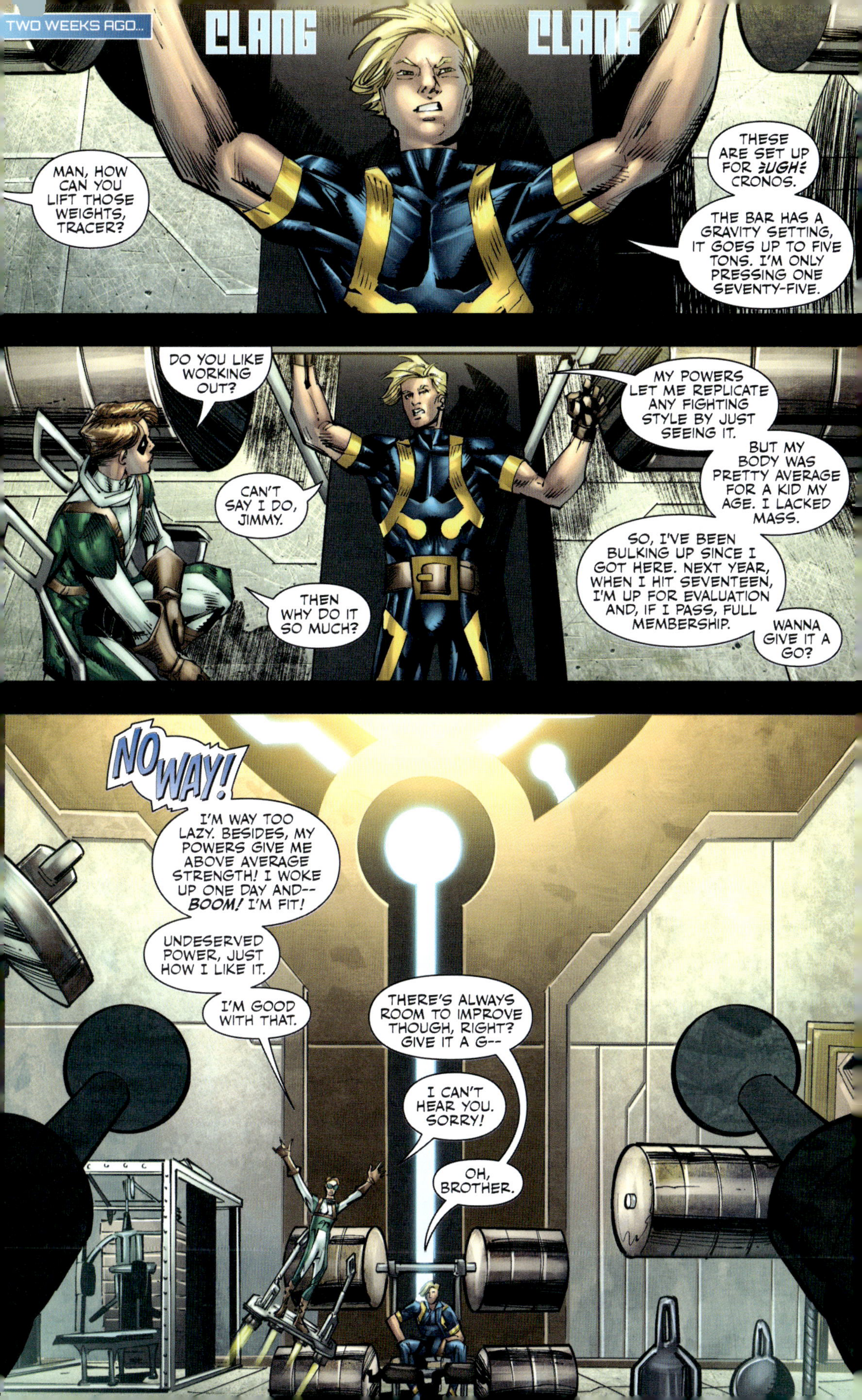
TWO WEEKS AGO...
CLANG
CLANG
MAN, HOW CAN YOU LIFT THOSE WEIGHTS, TRACER?
THESE ARE SET UP FOR ≷UGH≶ CRONOS.
THE BAR HAS A GRAVITY SETTING, IT GOES UP TO FIVE TONS. I'M ONLY PRESSING ONE SEVENTY-FIVE.
DO YOU LIKE WORKING OUT?
CAN'T SAY I DO, JIMMY.
THEN WHY DO IT SO MUCH?
MY POWERS LET ME REPLICATE ANY FIGHTING STYLE BY JUST SEEING IT.
BUT MY BODY WAS PRETTY AVERAGE FOR A KID MY AGE. I LACKED MASS.
SO, I'VE BEEN BULKING UP SINCE I GOT HERE. NEXT YEAR, WHEN I HIT SEVENTEEN, I'M UP FOR EVALUATION AND, IF I PASS, FULL MEMBERSHIP.
WANNA GIVE IT A GO?
NO WAY!
I'M WAY TOO LAZY. BESIDES, MY POWERS GIVE ME ABOVE AVERAGE STRENGTH! I WOKE UP ONE DAY AND-- ***BOOM!*** I'M FIT!
UNDESERVED POWER, JUST HOW I LIKE IT.
I'M GOOD WITH THAT.
THERE'S ALWAYS ROOM TO IMPROVE THOUGH, RIGHT? GIVE IT A G--
I CAN'T HEAR YOU. SORRY!
OH, BROTHER.

STORM
T.A.P. ROOM MAJOR
TRAINING, ASSESSMENT, AND PREPARATION.
I'LL CATCH YOU LATER!
STORM SURGE
COLORS
CORTEZ · GEORGE
LETTERS
WEATHERS
EDITOR
MALIN

3 DAYS AGO...

SAINT IGNACE HOSPITAL

BEEP-BEEP BEEP-BEEP

M-MARIA?

MAMA. I'M HERE.

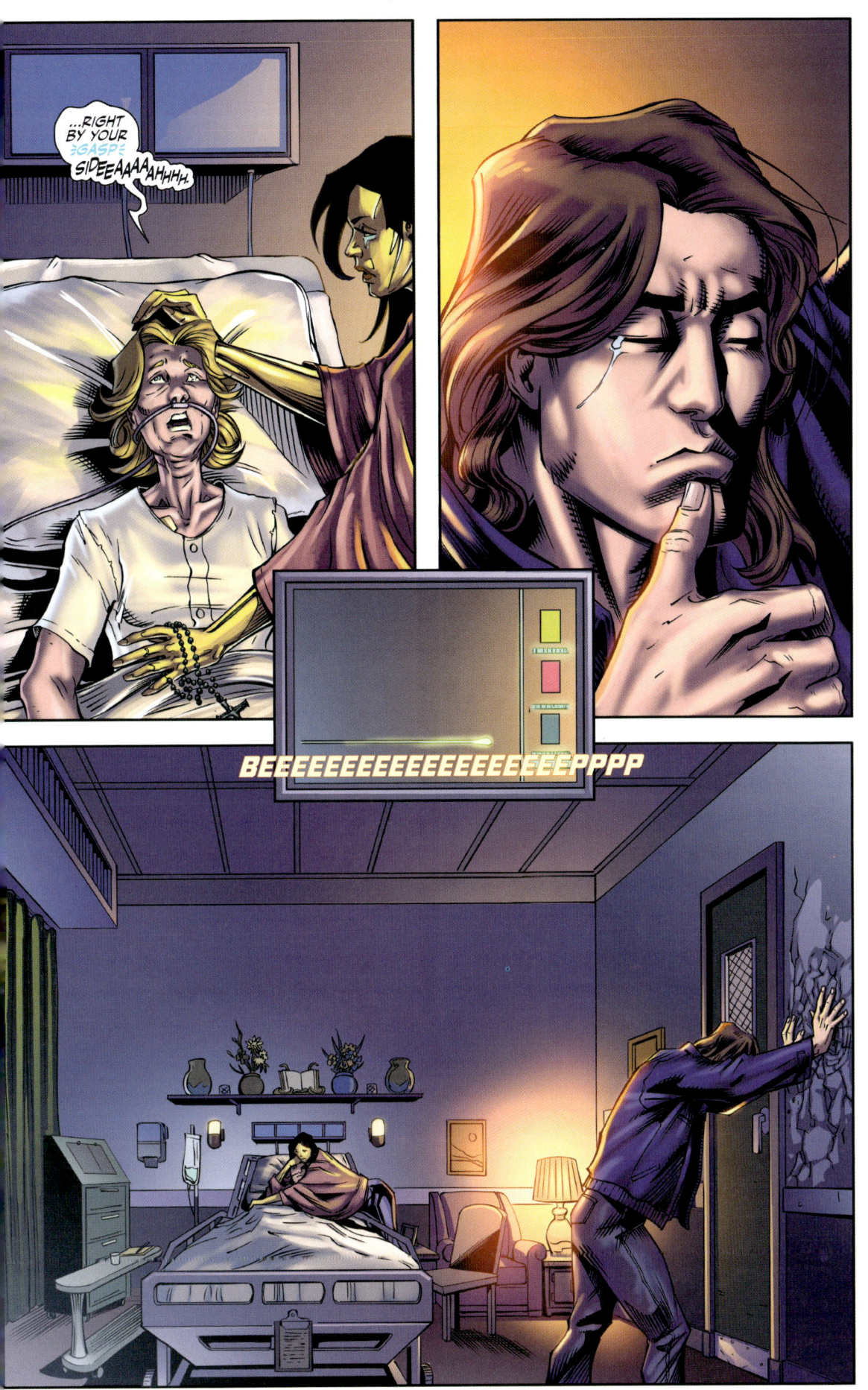

ALMOST THERE!

HE'S IN POSITION! CLEAR! LIGHT HIM UP!

NOW, HI-FI!

FIRING!

HAWHAW HAWHAW

Y'ALL NEVER MET A NIGGA LIKE ME!

"RUINER."

WHO ARE YOU?

WHAT JUST HAPPENED HERE?

MY NAME IS GENOA. I COME FROM A CONQUERED WORLD CALLED CAPPIA.

OUR INVADERS, THE DARR, RELIGIOUSLY SERVE A MASTER THEY CALL THE BLACK EMPEROR.

THEY NOW SPREAD WAR ACROSS GALAXIES, MURDERING ALL LIFE.

THREE MONTHS AGO I TRACKED A DARRIAN SMUGGLER, CALLED NIXX, TO EARTH.

NIXX BROUGHT CAPPIAN SUPERCHARGER TECHNOLOGY, WHICH WAS USED HERE, TO TRANSFORM YOUR MOST POWERFUL TRAITORS--

--SO THEY CAN KILL AS MANY SUPER POWERED THREATS AS POSSIBLE. CLEARING THE WAY.

ROAD RUNNER SAID THERE WERE EIGHT OF THESE SUPERCHARGERS.

COULD THERE BE MORE?

BEFORE MY PEOPLE LOST THE WAR, WE DESTROYED ALL KNOWN SUPERCHARGER TECH AND RESEARCH FACILITIES.

47 SUPERCHARGERS WERE UNACCOUNTED FOR. COUNTING THESE THREE, I'VE RECOVERED 41.

IF THERE ARE FIVE MORE HERE, I NEED TO FIND THEM.

BEFORE **MORE** PEOPLE DIE.

DUDE, ARE YOU **SHRINKING?**

POWERING DOWN. IF WE STAY IN OUR SUPERCHARGED FORMS TOO LONG, IT BECOMES PAINFUL.

IT TAKES JUST A BIT OF FOCUS.

THIS IS MY *TRUE* FORM. CAPPIANS WERE ONCE FROM EARTH.

OUR ANCESTORS ARE WHAT YOU CALL "ABDUCTEES."

THEY WERE TAKEN FROM THEIR LANDS TO THE STARS, STUDIED, ENSLAVED, AND EVENTUALLY FOUGHT FOR THEIR FREEDOM.

WE FOUND A NEW HOME. *CAPPIA.* SHE WAS VERY BEAUTIFUL.

NOW, I'M HERE TO BLEED OUT THE ENEMY.

THIS MAN IS ABSOLUTELY *GORGEOUS.* HIS NATURAL VOICE IS GIVING ME CHILLS.

HOW DO I GET SOME OF THAT?

SOME OF WHAT?

I--UH-- *NOTHING,* GENOA. I'M--NEVERMIND.

TRACER HERE. WE'RE GETTING A NEWS FEED FROM PRESIDENT SEWARD'S PRESS CONFERENCE.

YOU'LL WANT TO SEE THIS.

PATCH IT THROUGH.

--AS MANY OF YOU SUSPECTED, THE INCIDENT AT KEYSTONE LAKE WAS A DANGEROUS ALIEN ADVANCE ON OUR PLANET--*

--AN ACT OF WAR.

THE RUSSIANS SAY THAT THESE ALIENS VIEW US AS DEFENSELESS AS A NEWBORN. THAT WE SHOULD NEGOTIATE.

*YOU CAN FIND THE BATTLE OF KEYSTONE IN GRAVEYARD SHIFT VOL IV. TRUST ME! WOLF HOWL! AWOOOOOOOOOOO -JON!

I SAY, "NO." THE WORLD SAYS, "NO." THIS IS OUR PLANET. IF THESE MURDEROUS ALIEN SCUM WANT IT, THEY HAVE TO TAKE IT!

WE MUST LEARN FROM THE MISTAKES OF OUR ANCESTORS, THOSE CAUGHT OFF GUARD BY SUPERIOR TECHNOLOGY.

WHEN AT A DISADVANTAGE, WE MUST PULL TOGETHER AND STRIKE HARDER AND FASTER THAN THE ENEMY IS PREPARED FOR. NOT LINGER ABOUT, DISORGANIZED AND INDECISIVE.

IF THIS SHOULD BE HUMANITY'S END, THEN LET IT BE ONE OF FURY! WE WILL FORTIFY OUR PLANET AND SAFEGUARD OUR PEOPLE.

WITH THE COOPERATION OF GRAVEYARD SHIFT, WE WILL BOARD ALL WILLING OMEGAS AND THOUSANDS OF THE WORLD'S BEST TROOPS ONTO THEIR SHIP FOR A NEW ODYSSEY.

WE WILL MEET OUR WOULD-BE DESTROYERS, NOT WHERE THEY EXPECT US MOST, BUT WHERE THEY EXPECT US LEAST, AMONG THE STARS.

THIS WILL NOT BE EASY. MANY WILL NOT RETURN. IN THREE DAYS, WE JOURNEY TO THE STARS.

MAY GOD BLESS THESE MEN, THE UNITED STATES OF AMERICA, AND ALL THE PEOPLE OF OUR BELOVED PLANET EARTH.

IF I WANTED TO MURDER A BUNCH OF SUPER POWERED BEINGS--

"...AND THERE IT IS, FOLKS. PRESIDENT SEWARD HAS OFFICIALLY WELCOMED BACK RICK ROGERS AND ENLISTED OMEGA STORM TO REPRESENT THE NATIONS OF THE WORLD, ALL ON THE SAME DAY.

THE PEOPLE OF EARTH HAVEN'T BEEN THIS UNIVERSALLY EXCITED SINCE THE EAGLES REUNITED IN NINETY-FOUR. OVER TO YOU, JESSICA."

GEORGE BYRON
Channel 4 HLL

"#CONSPIRACY! YESTERDAY, WHILE INBOUND TO BELLEVUE HOSPITAL, THE AMBULANCE CARRYING ROAD RUNNER WAS BRUTALLY ATTACKED BY WHAT WITNESSES DESCRIBE AS FIVE LARGE HUMANOIDS. ALL ABOARD WERE SLAUGHTERED. WHAT DID ROAD RUNNER KNOW? WHAT IS OMEGA STORM HIDING?

"IN OTHER NEWS, RUMORS ARE SWIRLING THAT CERTIFIED ADULTERER LILITH MAYHEW, OR AS SOME CALL HER, 'THE WHORE BRIDE,' HAS BEEN REPORTED AS A PRISONER OF WAR. CAN YOU SAY #NOTMYPROBLEM?"

CHANNEL 64 NYUK
#HASHTAG

"HERE, WE SEE THE LAST OF THE PASSENGERS RECEIVING A NEURAL IMPLANT BEHIND THEIR RIGHT EAR, DESIGNED TO INTERRUPT OPTICAL SIGNALS TO THE BRAIN. WITHOUT IT, THEY SAY, VIEWING SOME OF THESE 'OLD GODS' WOULD DRIVE THE HUMAN MIND INSANE.

"OH--I'M BEING TOLD THAT CAPTAIN BLUD IS ON HIS WAY..."

LIVE
7 Chloe Kunnel

"THANKS, GEORGE. THE OFFICIAL WHITE HOUSE PRESS RELEASE STATES THAT INTERIM LEADER PSION IS STEPPING AWAY FROM OMEGA STORM DUTIES. HE WILL NOW ACT AS FIRST OFFICER, SECOND-IN-COMMAND TO THE FORMER TERRORIST VLADIMIR BLUD, WHO NOW HOLDS THE OFFICIAL RANK OF CAPTAIN UNDER NEW INTERNATIONAL PARTNERSHIPS."

Jessica De La Cruz
Channel 4 HLL

"AN HOUR AGO, THIS ABSOLUTELY MASSIVE FORTRESS, DUBBED BY THE PRESS AS 'CASTLE DRACULA,' LAUNCHED WITH 10,000 SOULS, COMPRISING OF SOLDIERS, SUPERHUMANS, ENGINEERS, COOKS, AND MORE, TO THE STARS.

"GODSPEED AND GOD BLESS AMERICA."

6 JOSHUA MORGUE
Breaking News!

"...AND THERE HE IS. I CAN'T TELL YOU HOW MUCH ENERGY IS IN THE ROOM RIGHT NOW. IT'S OVERWHELMING. CAPTAIN BLUD IS A ROCKSTAR TO MOST OF THESE MEN, HAVING SERVED WITH THEM ON THE STILL SECRETIVE MISSION IN ANTARCTICA.

"NOW, LEADING THE MOST IMPORTANT MISSION IN THE HISTORY OF MANKIND, TO THE--"

STORM

"IT SEEMED LIKE THE ENTIRE WORLD WAS AGAINST HIM.

"AS BILL SHAKESPEARE ONCE WROTE IN HIS LATER YEARS, 'MISERY ACQUAINTS A MAN WITH STRANGE BEDFELLOWS'."

DOWNTIME

COLORS
GEORGE

LETTERS
WEATHERS

EDITOR
MALIN

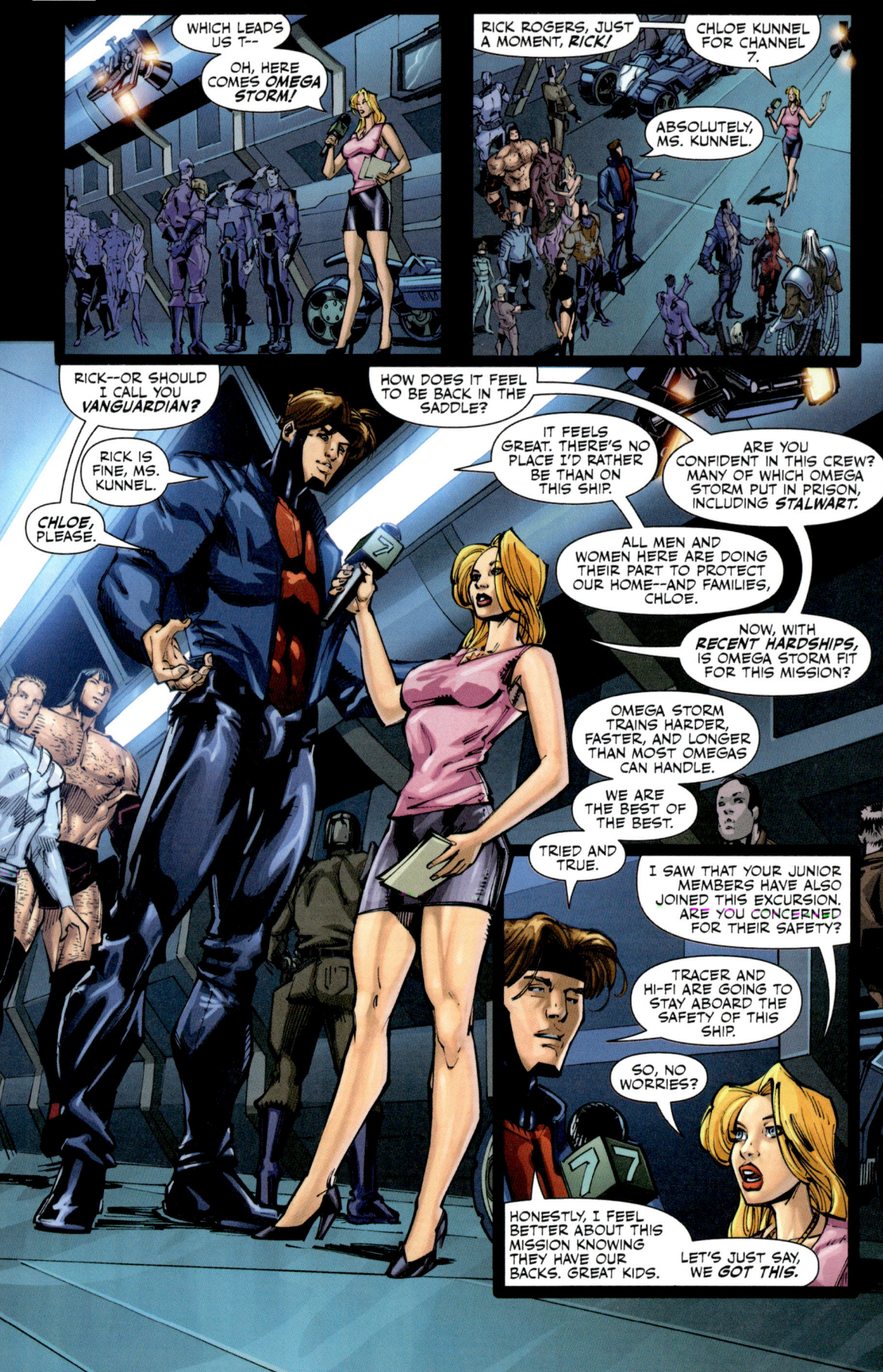

YAAAWWWN

GOOD TIMES.

'NOS, LOOK AT THAT DUDE OVER THERE, *BRAM*. I BET HE'S GOT A *HUGE HOG.*

WHAT'S WITH YOU AND *DICKS?*

CRAM IT, 'NOS!

SCIENCE *RUN AMOK* GAVE YOU A FREAKIN' TANK BODY, HOUSING HOGZILLA!

A *BLESSING* AND A *CURSE*, BRUH. MOST CHICKS SEE MY JUNK AND *RUN FOR THEIR LIVES.*

ONLY *RASPUTIN* KNOWS YOUR PAIN.

HUGE HOG.

THEY CUT IT OFF AND PRESERVED IT IN A JAR--*FOR SCIENCE.*

SAME FOR YOU. *TRUST* ME.

I CURSE MY DAD EVERY DAY FOR THESE GOOD LOOKS AND THIS SMALL YET AESTHETICALLY PLEASING FRAME AND PEEN.

HEY, WHERE ALL THE *WHITE WOMEN* AT? OR, *ANY WOMEN?* THIS PLACE IS *DRY AS TOAST.*

THIS IS A ONE YEAR TRIP, *MINIMUM.* WE NEED TO SECURE SOME *TAIL* BEFORE THIS SHIP TURNS INTO A *GAY STAR TREK.*

DUUUUDE, YOU ARE SO FREAKIN' RIGHT. IT'S GONNA GET WEIRD AROUND HERE, BRUH.

WHEN WE WRAP, WE'RE GONNA STRUT DOWN THAT HALL AND FIND SOME TOAST TO BUTTER, AMIGO.

THANK YOU, MS. KUNNEL, BUT MR. ROGERS HAS A MEETING WITH *CAPTAIN BLUD.*

WE'D BE DELIGHTED TO TALK MORE AFTER WE ALL GET SETTLED IN.

I--UH--THANK YOU FOR YOUR TIME, RICK.

MY PLEASURE, CHLOE. HAVE A *GREAT* DAY.

...CUT.

TRANSMISSION ENDED.

UMMMM--

ARE YOU FEELING *UNWELL?*

HOLY DUCK. IT WASN'T *THAT* OBVIOUS WAS IT?

MY SCANNERS SHOW AN INCREASE IN PULSE, BODY TEMPERATURE, HUMIDITY AND PHEROMON--

STOP!

PLEASE STOP.

NOW, DIRECTOR HUNT THINKS WE MIGHT HAVE *FIVE* REALLY BIG PROBLEMS ABOARD MY SHIP.

SUPERCHARGERS?

THAT IS POSSIBLE, CAPTAIN.

I'VE ASSIGNED OUR JUNIOR MEMBERS, *TRACER* AND *HI-FI*, TO FAMILIARIZE THEMSELVES WITH YOUR SECURITY SYSTEMS.

THEY'RE BRIGHT BOYS.

HI-FI WAS CRACKING SECURE PENTAGON SYSTEMS WHEN HE WAS ONLY *NINE* YEARS OLD.

PERFECT. ALLOW ME TO INTRODUCE OUR *OWN* TECH GENIUS...

HARKER. UPDATE.

GOOD DAY, GENTLEMEN.

--THAT WON'T HAPPEN HERE, I ASSURE YOU.

FOR THE LAST 48 HOURS, THE NSA HAS BEEN SENDING OVER 400 TERABYTES OF DATA FROM THE THREE ALIEN SUPERCHARGERS.

THE TECHNOLOGY IS FAR, FAR BEYOND US. AS ARTHUR C. CLARKE SAID, IT IS LIKE "MAGIC."

HYPOTHESIS?

CONSIDERING THEIR EXPELLED ENERGY SIGNATURES...

...THE SUPERCHARGER IS IDENTICAL TO THE "CURSED" BELL THAT BRAM'S FRIEND, J-MAN, CARRIES FROM THEIR ALTERNATE UNIVERSE.

SAME TOOL, DIFFERENT REALITIES.

WHAT WE SEE IN OUR UNIVERSE IS JUST A SMALLER PART OF A MASSIVE, UNKNOWN "MACHINE" IN ANOTHER. THE SOURCE.

AS FOR LOCATING THE DEVICES--

--ALL SHIP SCANS READ NEGATIVE, EVEN FOR THE SUPERCHARGER CARRIED BY YOUR GUEST GENOA.

IF WE DO FIND UNAUTHORIZED TECHNOLOGICAL WEAPONS ARE ACTIVATED, THEN THE SHIP WILL AUTOMATICALLY TELEPORT IT AND ITS WIELDER INTO SPACE IN UNDER A SECOND.

WE'VE ALLOWED THIS INFORMATION TO SPREAD.

NOTED.

THAT IS ALL, HARKER.

I SHALL REPORT ANY :BZZZT: ANOMALIES. ADIEU.

RICK, THE OLD ONE'S MONOLITH IS OUR MAP TO THEIR HOMEWORLD, BUT A SMALL *UNKNOWN* PLANET HOLDS A HELPFUL COMPONENT.

WITH IT, WE CAN SHAVE TWENTY DAYS FROM OUR JOURNEY, GIVING US AN INCREDIBLE EDGE.

TO RECOVER IT, I MAY NEED YOUR TEAM TO JOIN TWO OTHERS FOR A *SNATCH AND GRAB*.

BE PREPARED.

WE'LL BE READY, CAPTAIN.

I'LL LET YOU AND OMEGA STORM HANDLE THE SUPERCHARGER INVESTIGATION. HARKER IS AT YOUR DISPOSAL.

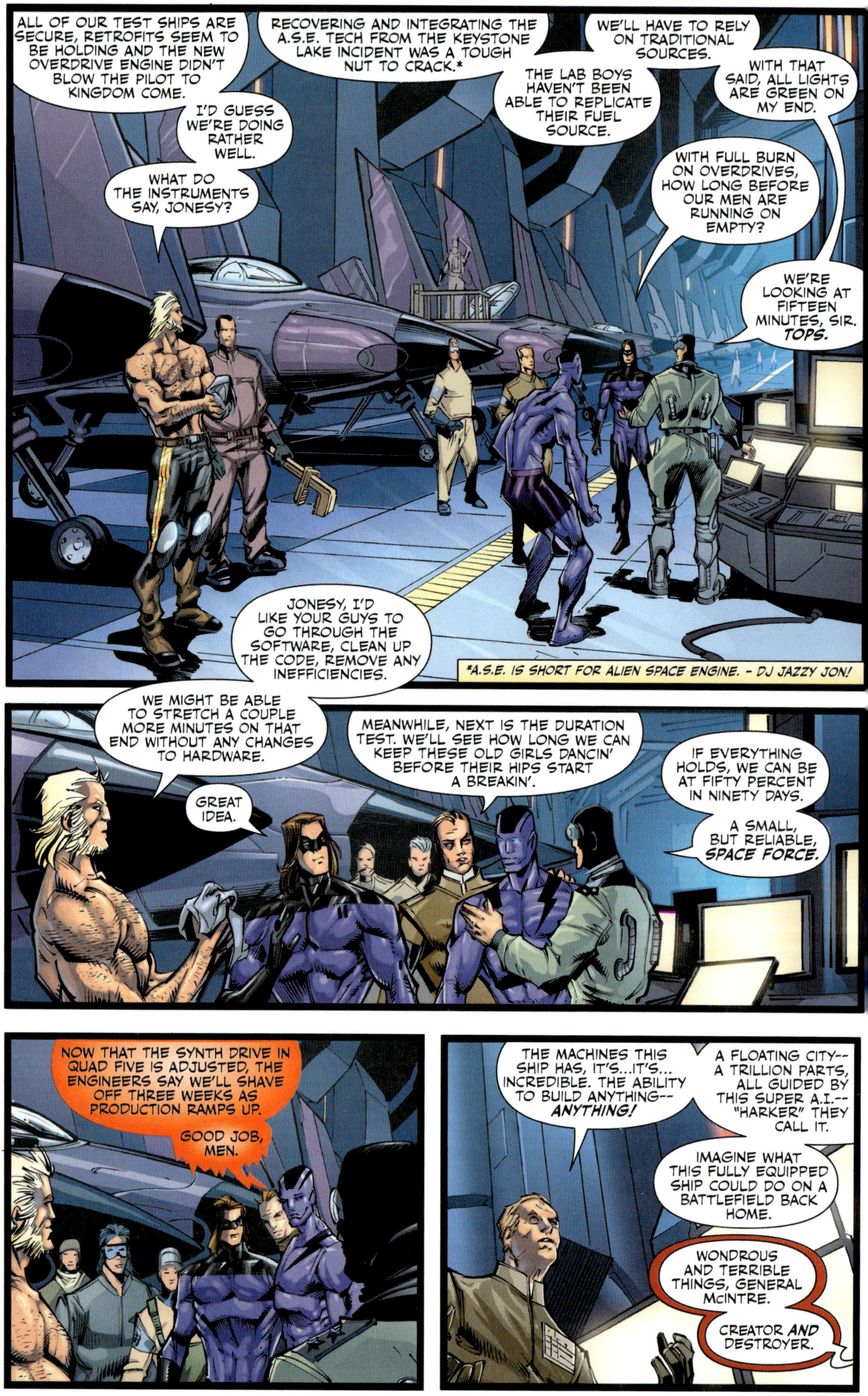

ALL OF OUR TEST SHIPS ARE SECURE, RETROFITS SEEM TO BE HOLDING AND THE NEW OVERDRIVE ENGINE DIDN'T BLOW THE PILOT TO KINGDOM COME.

I'D GUESS WE'RE DOING RATHER WELL.

WHAT DO THE INSTRUMENTS SAY, JONESY?

RECOVERING AND INTEGRATING THE A.S.E. TECH FROM THE KEYSTONE LAKE INCIDENT WAS A TOUGH NUT TO CRACK.*

THE LAB BOYS HAVEN'T BEEN ABLE TO REPLICATE THEIR FUEL SOURCE.

WE'LL HAVE TO RELY ON TRADITIONAL SOURCES.

WITH THAT SAID, ALL LIGHTS ARE GREEN ON MY END.

WITH FULL BURN ON OVERDRIVES, HOW LONG BEFORE OUR MEN ARE RUNNING ON EMPTY?

WE'RE LOOKING AT FIFTEEN MINUTES, SIR. *TOPS.*

JONESY, I'D LIKE YOUR GUYS TO GO THROUGH THE SOFTWARE, CLEAN UP THE CODE, REMOVE ANY INEFFICIENCIES.

*A.S.E. IS SHORT FOR ALIEN SPACE ENGINE. — DJ JAZZY JON!

WE MIGHT BE ABLE TO STRETCH A COUPLE MORE MINUTES ON THAT END WITHOUT ANY CHANGES TO HARDWARE.

GREAT IDEA.

MEANWHILE, NEXT IS THE DURATION TEST. WE'LL SEE HOW LONG WE CAN KEEP THESE OLD GIRLS DANCIN' BEFORE THEIR HIPS START A BREAKIN'.

IF EVERYTHING HOLDS, WE CAN BE AT FIFTY PERCENT IN NINETY DAYS.

A SMALL, BUT RELIABLE, *SPACE FORCE.*

NOW THAT THE SYNTH DRIVE IN QUAD FIVE IS ADJUSTED, THE ENGINEERS SAY WE'LL SHAVE OFF THREE WEEKS AS PRODUCTION RAMPS UP.

GOOD JOB, MEN.

THE MACHINES THIS SHIP HAS, IT'S...IT'S... INCREDIBLE. THE ABILITY TO BUILD ANYTHING-- *ANYTHING!*

A FLOATING CITY-- A TRILLION PARTS, ALL GUIDED BY THIS SUPER A.I.-- "HARKER" THEY CALL IT.

IMAGINE WHAT THIS FULLY EQUIPPED SHIP COULD DO ON A BATTLEFIELD BACK HOME.

WONDROUS AND TERRIBLE THINGS, GENERAL McINTRE.

CREATOR *AND* DESTROYER.

THIS *SUCKS.* THESE OLD GUYS PUSHED US OFF INTO THE KIDS CORNER.

I'M ALMOST *FIFTEEN,* YA KNOW!

THIS IS THE MOST IMPORTANT FIGHT OF OUR *LIVES.*

WE SHOULD BE WITH OMEGA STORM!

I WANT IN ON THE ACTION TOO, *HI-FI.*

MY DAD FREAKED WHEN HE HEARD I WAS LEAVING FOR THIS MISSION.

BUT HE UNDERSTANDS, IT'S AN HONOR TO BE HERE.

WE'LL DO OUR BEST TO CONTRIBUTE, EVEN IF THAT MEANS GRABBING A MOP AND BROOM.

WELL, I'M GLAD *YOUR* DAD TOOK IT SO WELL.

MY PARENTS HAVEN'T BEEN MISSING ME ONE BIT SINCE MY POWERS DEVELOPED LAST YEAR.

JUST BECAUSE I *ACCIDENTALLY* BLEW UP THE DOG HOUSE.

THEY'D HOLD A GRUDGE FOR *THAT?*

WELL, THE DOG WAS IN IT...MR. PICKLES.

WHAT?!

YEAH. THEY LOVED THAT DOG.

...

IT JUST BOTHERS ME THAT WE AREN'T SITTING AT THE ADULT TABLE. WE'RE SMARTER THAN THESE OLD DUDES BUT ONE STEP FROM TAKING OUT THE TRASH.

SO WE PROVE OURSELVES, EARN THEIR RESPECT.

MY TABLET!

OOPS!

GAH!

I GOT IT!

BAH! OH, DID YOU HEAR ABOUT THIS DANGER BAY ON--

I DON'T KNOW, I KIND OF *LIKE* THAT NAME.

SOOOO, TRACER? DO YOU TURN TRACED PHOTOS INTO LIVING CREATURES OR SOMETHING LIKE THAT?

MY DAD USED TO MAKE ME WATCH THIS CARTOON WHERE THESE HOLOGRAMS CAME TO LIFE, THERE WAS THIS COOL ARCHER GUY.

UH, YEAH. NOT EXACTLY, I CAN MASTER ANY WEAPON AND FIGHTING STYLE I SEE.

I FIND PATTERNS. IT COMES IN HANDY WITH THE TECH STUFF TOO.

AH, I SEE YOU THREE, AH, MET. EXCELLENT.

HELLO, DR. PRIDE.

I'M TURNING FIFTEEN NEXT MONTH.

HI, DAD.

YES, YES, IF I MAY HAVE YOUR ATTENTION FOR, AH, JUST A MOMENT, GENTLEMEN AND, AH, LADY...

WE ARE CURRENTLY APPROACHING THE, AH, WORMHOLE, OFFICIALLY NAMED, SBOO1.

SBOO1?

AH, YES, THE 001 REPRESENTS THE FIRST WORMHOLE THIS SHIP HAS NAMED ON BEHALF OF EARTH AND THE, AH, "SB" IS FOR MY FAVORITE, AH, ACTOR, *STEVE BUSCEMI.*

STEVE BUSCEMI?

YES, STEVE BUSCEMI.

WE BELIEVE THAT *WORMHOLE BUSCEMI* WILL HAVE LITTLE EFFECT ON THIS SHIP OVERALL...

...BUT, MUCH LIKE IT'S NAMESAKE, MAY, AH, GIVE US A HIGHLY SURPRISING, AND, AH, MEMORABLE SCENE STEALING PERFORMANCE.

SO, AH, YES, I NEED YOU THREE TO TAKE A SEAT AND BUCKLE UP JUST IN CASE.

WHY NOT TRAVOLTA? WILLIS?

ENOUGH, HI-FI.

I KINDA LIKE BUSCEMI.

I'LL BE *RIGHT* OVER HERE IF YOU NEED ME, KIDS.

"KIDS"!

IT'LL BE ALRIGHT, HI-FI.

YOU'LL SEE.

AWWW, MAN. WHAT'S WRONG WITH ME? IT MUST BE THE SHIP, THE SECLUSION--

BE COOL, ERIC. DON'T LET IT SHOW OR HI-FI WILL KNOW THAT--

I'M HEAD OVER HEELS FOR YOU, JENNY PRIDE.

HERE WE GO!

ONE HOUR LATER...

"ALL SYSTEMS HAVE STABILIZED, CAPTAIN BLUD.

WE HAVE FORTY SIX PEOPLE WOUNDED, THREE CRITICAL. NO FATALITIES AS OF YET.

WE'VE FOUND NO CLEAR EVIDENCE OF SABOTAGE AND BELIEVE IT TO BE A RANDOM ENERGY DISCHARGE FROM THE WORMHOLE WALL.

CAPTAIN! HEAT SENSORS ARE GOING WAY UP! WE'RE NEARING THE EXIT.

THE PLANET HAS A SINGULAR SURFACE ANAMOLY, A STRUCTURE...

SCANNERS ARE SHOWING A NEARBY PLANET IN EXTREME PROXIMITY TO THIS SYSTEM'S SUN.

...IT MATCHES THE DESCRIPTION FROM THE MONOLITH, IT'S OUR TARGET.

VLAD, IF WE CAN DETECT THEM, THEY MAY BE DETECTING US.

HARKER, ACTIVATE THE CLOAKING SYSTEM!

POSITION THE CASTLE IN ORBIT ON THE NIGHT SIDE, BRING US INTO THE RING SYSTEM FOR CONCEALMENT AND COVER.

INCREASE SHIELDS TO BLOCK ANY ADDITIONAL RADIATION--

D-D-DEBOCYLE?!

WHY THE HELL ARE WE ORBITING *DEBOCYLE?!*

YOU *KNOW* THIS PLANET, ARC?

OH, YEAH, RICK. I SPENT *SIX MONTHS* IN THIS HELLHOLE!

THIS PLACE ALMOST BROKE ME.

IT'S PART TEMPLE, PART TORTURE CHAMBER, AND ALL PARTS PRISON.

TOTAL INSANITY. EVIL GUARDING EVIL.

THEY BRUTALIZE THE PRISONERS HERE. THEY THINK THAT SUFFERING WILL GIVE LIFE TO THIS GIANT ROCK GOD THEY CALLED *TOTH AGADA.*

THIS PRISON, *HELMSAGAHD,* IS RUN BY A CLASS-A PSYCHOPATH NAMED *PARROX.*

FREAKY DUDE. SADIST. HE CRUSHES HEADS LIKE GRAPES TO EASE BOREDOM. I SAW IT.

PROBABLY A TWENTY-FIVE ON THE KIRBY SCALE. WICKED AND MEAN AS ALL FREAKING HELL!

YOU ESCAPED. CAN YOU GET US IN?

ARE YOU NOT LISTENING? THAT PLACE IS A *DEATH* TRAP!

AND?

≥SIGH≤ WE COULD POSSIBLY ENTER THE WAY I EXITED... BUT WE NEED CODE BREAKERS-- TO ACCESS SECURE UNITS.

THE CODES EXPIRE EVERY EIGHTY EIGHT DAYS. ONE DEBOCYLE ORBIT AROUND ITS SUN.

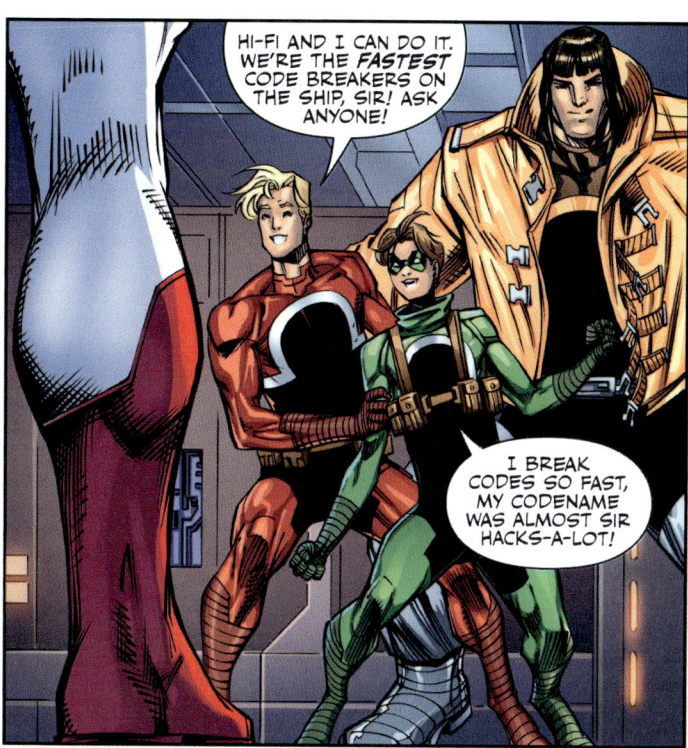

HI-FI AND I CAN DO IT. WE'RE THE *FASTEST* CODE BREAKERS ON THE SHIP, SIR! ASK ANYONE!

I BREAK CODES SO FAST, MY CODENAME WAS ALMOST SIR HACKS-A-LOT!

BOYS, I THINK IT'S BEST TO KEEP YOU SAFE HERE-- FOR NOW.

SIR, WE'RE NOT JUST ANY TECH GUYS, WE'RE *OMEGA STORM*.

WE KNOW WHAT'S ON THE LINE. WE KNOW THE PLAYS AND SAFE ZONES.

GIVE US A *SHOT*, SIR. PLEASE.

WE'LL BREAK THE CODES AND STAY SAFELY OUT OF SIGHT UNTIL YOU NEED US. JUST GIVE US A CHANCE TO PROVE OURSELVES.

HI-FI AND I WON'T LET THE TEAM OR THE MISSION DOWN.

WE'RE AN ASSET.

WELL--YOU'RE RIGHT, MEN. FROM THIS DAY ON, YOU ARE NOW ACTIVE DUTY MEMBERS OF OMEGA STORM.

WE FIGHT AS PROMISED--

TOGETHER.

YEAH!

WELCOME ABOARD, GUYS!

IT WAS NICE KNOWING YA.

BRUH, CHILL!

ARC DOESN'T MEAN IT.

PSION WILL TAKE ARC TO VLAD FOR A DEBRIEF. I'LL MEET EVERYONE IN HANGAR BAY 7 TOMORROW AT EXACTLY ZERO SEVEN HUNDRED HOURS.

EVERYONE SHOWS UP EARLY, NO ONE SHOWS UP LATE.

CHECK YOUR BUDDY.

GET YOUR THINGS IN ORDER TONIGHT, TEAM. I NEED YOU TO SHOW UP WITH ALL THE PHYSICAL, EMOTIONAL, AND SPIRITUAL FITNESS YOU HAVE TOMORROW. POSITIVE ENERGY. COMMITTED TO ONLY TWO THINGS--

VICTORY AND GETTING ALL OF US BACK HERE, ALIVE.

GOOD LUCK, EVERYONE. THAT WILL BE ALL.

WELCOME ABOARD, BOYS.

THIS IS MY CHANCE TO PROVE MY METTLE.

RICK! RICK ROGERS! CHLOE KUNNEL, CHANNEL 7 NEWS!

OH, GOOD EVENING, CHLOE.

CAN I HAVE JUST A FEW MINUTES OF YOUR TIME, RICK?

SURE. FOLLOW ME.

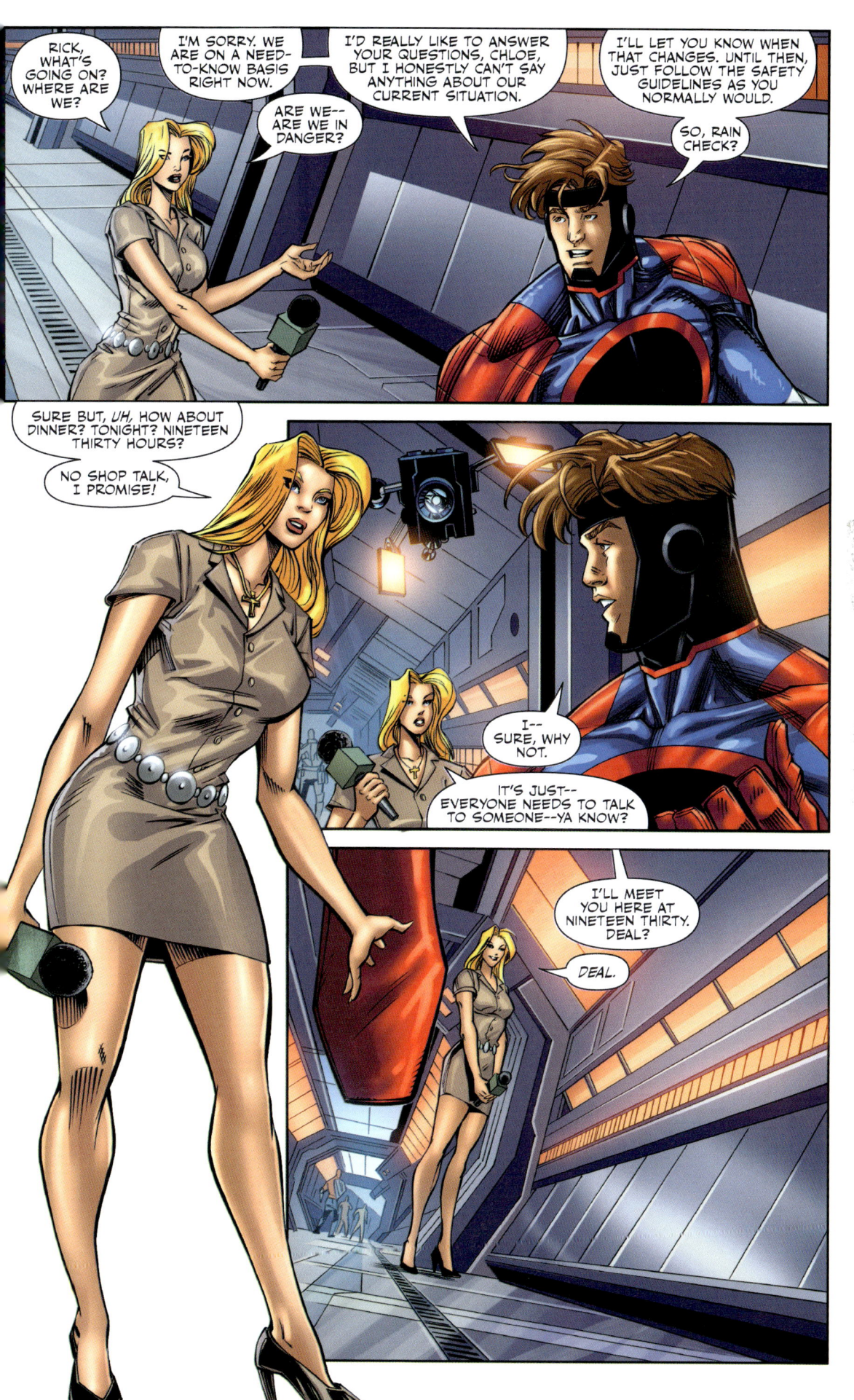

WELCOME, RED TEAM.

WE'VE DISCOVERED THAT THE COMPONENT WE SEEK IS A SIMPLE DISC THAT CONTAINS COORDINATES WHICH CREATES A SHORTCUT TO THE OLD ONES' HOMEWORLD.

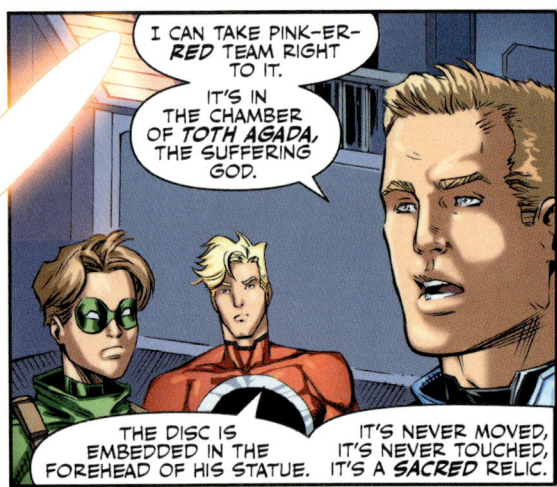

I CAN TAKE PINK—ER—*RED* TEAM RIGHT TO IT.

IT'S IN THE CHAMBER OF *TOTH AGADA*, THE SUFFERING GOD.

THE DISC IS EMBEDDED IN THE FOREHEAD OF HIS STATUE.

IT'S NEVER MOVED, IT'S NEVER TOUCHED, IT'S A *SACRED* RELIC.

RED TEAM WILL ENTER ONE OF SEVERAL SMALL DISCHARGE VENTS INTO HELMSAGAHD.

SECURE THE DISC, AND WORK OUR WAY TO THE SURFACE LEVEL FOR EXTRACTION.

EASY IN. EASY OUT.

PERHAPS. GOLD AND BLUE TEAMS WILL DRAW OUT ANY OPPOSITION THEY MIGHT FIND.

THEY'LL BE IN THE HIGHEST THREAT LEVEL IF OUR PLAN WORKS.

HEY, UH, MICK IS IT? I'M JACK, JACK STONE. NICE TO MEET YOU, UH, WHAT TEAM ARE WE ON? RED?

BLUE.

DAMN.

I'LL LEAD BLUE TEAM TO TAKE OUT ANY AND ALL COMMUNICATION DEVICES.

ONCE COMMS ARE DOWN WE WILL BEGIN A TOP DOWN SWEEP AND CLEAR. EVERY POSSIBLE THREAT DIES.

WHEN WE HIT GROUND LEVEL, WE WILL HOLD THE INTERIOR EXIT UNTIL RED TEAM IS PREPARED FOR EVAC.

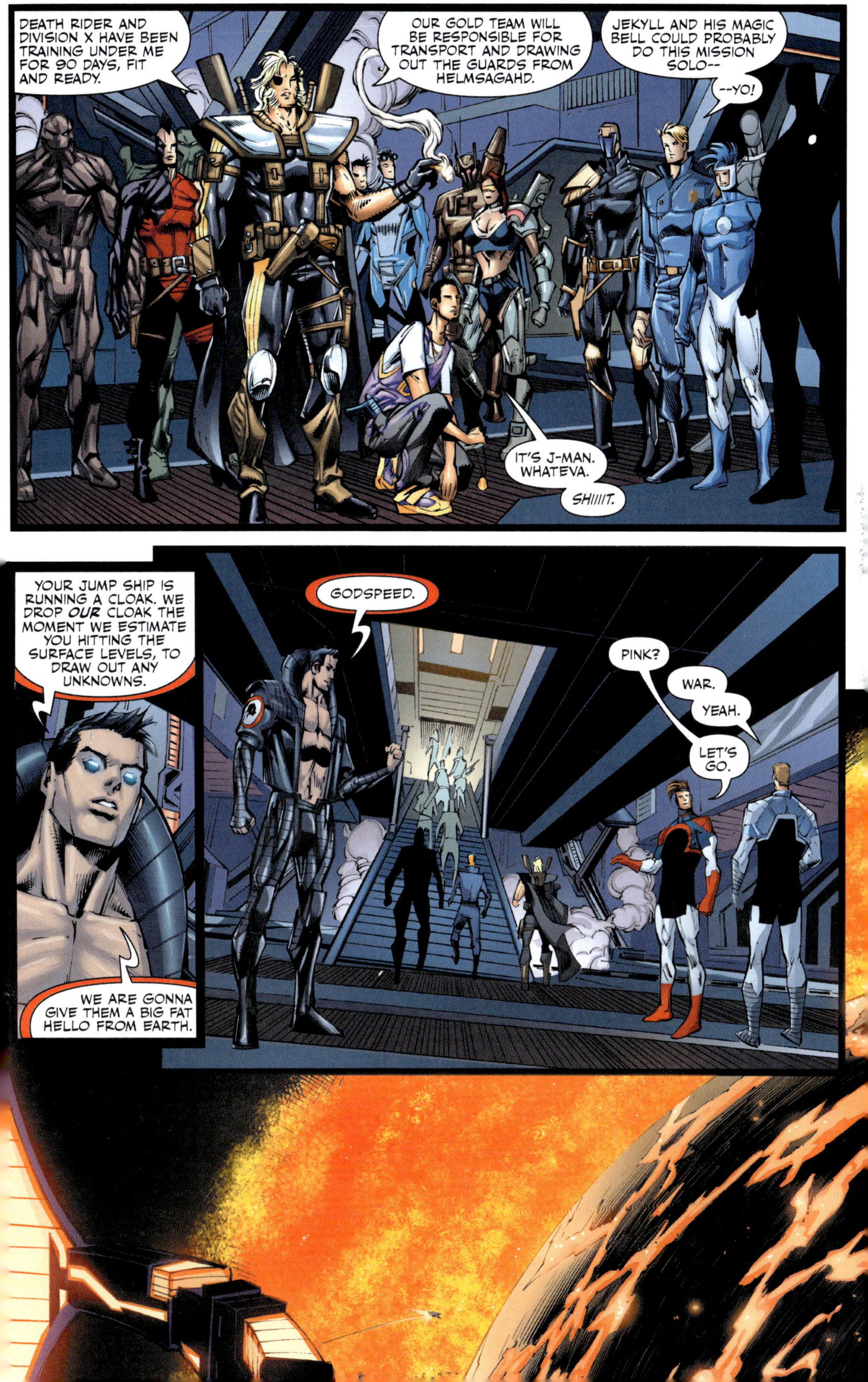

DEATH RIDER AND DIVISION X HAVE BEEN TRAINING UNDER ME FOR 90 DAYS, FIT AND READY.
OUR GOLD TEAM WILL BE RESPONSIBLE FOR TRANSPORT AND DRAWING OUT THE GUARDS FROM HELMSAGAHD.
JEKYLL AND HIS MAGIC BELL COULD PROBABLY DO THIS MISSION SOLO--
--YO!
IT'S J-MAN. WHATEVA.
SHIIIIT.
YOUR JUMP SHIP IS RUNNING A CLOAK. WE DROP OUR CLOAK THE MOMENT WE ESTIMATE YOU HITTING THE SURFACE LEVELS, TO DRAW OUT ANY UNKNOWNS.
WE ARE GONNA GIVE THEM A BIG FAT HELLO FROM EARTH.
GODSPEED.
PINK?
WAR.
YEAH.
LET'S GO.

"YO, VLAD MUST'VE DROPPED THE CLOAK. HERE THEY COME!"

THEY'RE GETTING AWFULLY CLOSE. WE COULD'VE BEEN SOLD OUT.

BY WHO?

ALL CLEAR. WE'RE GONNA RUN HOT AND LOW!

HOLD ON!

CLICK

"THAR SHE BLOWS!"

GO! GO!

WOOSH

TWENTY SECONDS LATER...

SOOO, WHERE'S THE MAINTENANCE HATCH?

UMMMMM. AH, I SEE IT!

I THINK.

...BRUH.

WE LOST FIVE MEN.

THAT'S NOT--

WHERE DID THEY GO? KILLED?

I DON'T THINK SO. THEY WERE RIGHT BEHIND ME.

NO BOOM.

NO SCREAMS.

NOTHING.

THAT DOESN'T MAKE SENS--

NO TIME TO WASTE. JACK STONE CAN USE OUR HELP! LET'S GO.

WE HAVE NINETY SECONDS UNTIL THE NEXT DISCHARGE.

HOW ARE WE LOOKING?

WE'RE ALMOST THERE, SIR.

WE HAD A LANGUAGE BARRIER WITH OUR INTERFACE, BUT WE'RE PAST THAT NOW.

THIS SHOULD DO IT.

DAMN.

CAN'T ONE OF YOU TOUGH GUYS JUST BREAK THIS DOOR IN?

WE COULD, BUT THEN IT WOULDN'T SEAL FOR THE DISCHARGE. HALF OF US WILL BE BLOWN TO BITS.

WHAT DOES THIS THING EVEN DO?

THINK, ERIC.

EVERYONE BACK UP!

OH, SNAP!

READY CRONOS! IN 3-2-1!

CAH-RASH

WATCH OUT!

≡COUGH≡ WELL--
≡COUGH≡ THAT
WORKED?

HELL
YEAH!

NOW IF I CAN
JUST FIND A
TALL GLASS
OF WAT--

WATCH YOUR
STEP!

LAVA
BATH.

WELL--
WE MADE
IT.

THIS IS
ONE TALL
ROOM.

IT HAS
TO BE--

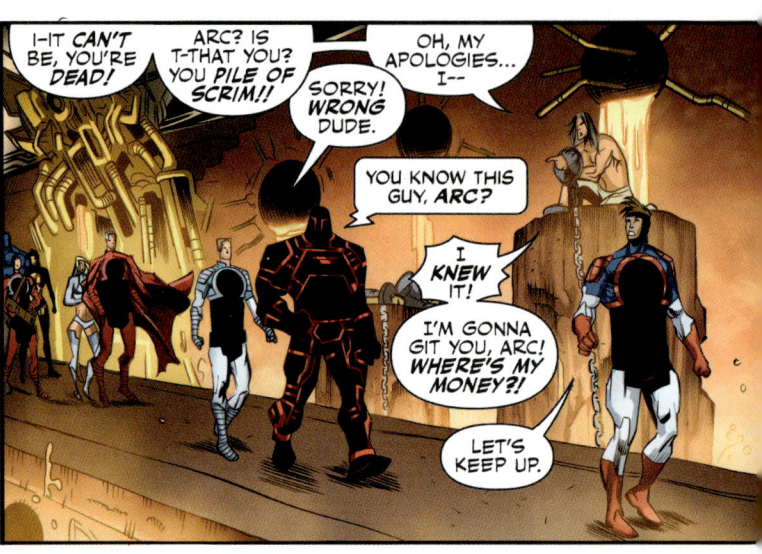

CHECK THESE GUYS OUT, *TOMMY.* THE ONLY THING STANDING BETWEEN THEM AND THAT DISC IS US.

VERY ASTUTE OF YOU, *CHROMEDOME.*

COME VA, *RICK?*

WHAT? YOU DON'T RECOGNIZE YOUR OLD FRIEND, *GARRA?*

WELL, IT HAS BEEN FIFTEEN YEARS SINCE YOU LOCKED ME AWAY IN OMEGA BLOCK.

FOR *FIFTEEN* YEARS I'VE DREAMED OF PUTTING MY TALONS THROUGH YOUR GUTS.

THOMAS "GARRA" SCAGNETTI. CROOKED COP TURNED COP KILLER. I NEVER FORGET YOUR KIND.

NOW, WHY AREN'T YOU WITH BLUE TEAM?!?

BECAUSE REVENGE SEEMS *SWEETER* IF I STAB HUMANITY IN THE BACK ALONG THE WAY.

LOOKING FOR *THESE?*

YOU WOULD SELL OUT YOUR OWN *PLANET?*

PEOPLE?

FOR *WHAT?*

I'M HAVING DEJA VU RIGHT NOW.

"AUSTRALIA." HA HA HA

HUMANS HAD OUR SHOT, VANGUARDIAN. IT'S TIME FOR US TO GET OUT OF THE FUCKING WAY.

WELL SAID, BRICK.

GREAT, FREAKING *NIHILISTS.* I HATE *WRIST CUTTERS.*

WHAT ARE WE GONNA DO, RICK?

RICK, I CAN'T PENETRATE THEIR MINDS. THEY'VE BEEN TRAINED FOR RESISTANCE.

STEADY...

THAT'S RIGHT, SALKA. WE KNOW HOW TO KEEP OUR MINDS FROM YOUR CONTROL.

ARRIVEDERCI, OMEGA STORM.

OMEGA STORM!

TAKE THEM OUT!

WHAP

WHAP

WHAP

DI QUI NON SI PASSA!

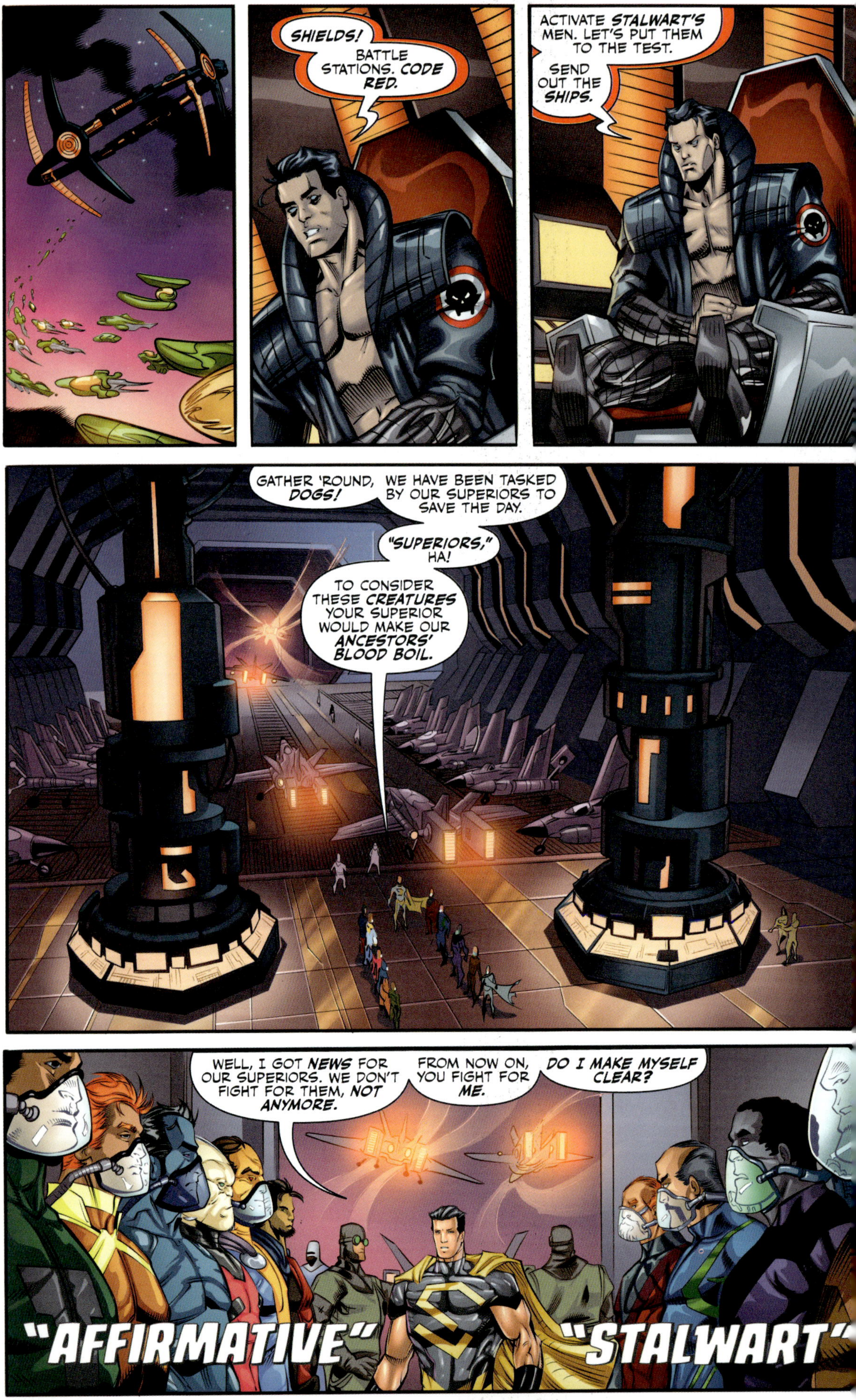

SHIELDS! BATTLE STATIONS. *CODE RED.*

ACTIVATE *STALWART'S* MEN. LET'S PUT THEM TO THE TEST. SEND OUT THE *SHIPS.*

GATHER 'ROUND, *DOGS!* WE HAVE BEEN TASKED BY OUR SUPERIORS TO SAVE THE DAY.

"SUPERIORS," HA!

TO CONSIDER THESE *CREATURES* YOUR SUPERIOR WOULD MAKE OUR *ANCESTORS'* BLOOD BOIL.

WELL, I GOT *NEWS* FOR OUR SUPERIORS. WE DON'T FIGHT FOR THEM, *NOT ANYMORE.*

FROM NOW ON, YOU FIGHT FOR *ME.*

DO I MAKE MYSELF CLEAR?

"AFFIRMATIVE"   "STALWART"

WHAT ARE MY THREE LAWS?

THE WEAK SERVE THE STRONG.

THE STRONGEST MUST ALWAYS LEAD.

ALL OPPOSITION TO LAW ONE AND TWO MUST BE DESTROYED.

YOU WERE ONCE LIKE THEM-- *PATRONIZED* AND *PACIFIED* WITH WORDS LIKE *"HERO."* PRAISED FOR YOUR NOBLE SERVICES AND YOUR DESIRES FOR NOTHING IN RETURN.

UNTIL I INTRODUCED A SIMPLE TRUTH.

THAT YOU WERE A *DOG.* USED BY SELF-APPOINTED SHEPHERDS TO *CONTROL* AND *PROTECT* THE SHEEP FROM WHICH THEY PROFIT.

WAGGING YOUR TAIL *BELOW* THEM, INSTEAD OF *GNASHING* YOUR TEETH ABOVE.

SHAMED FROM WANTING TO SHARE IN THE *POWER* AND *WEALTH* THAT YOU CREATED, WITH THE SHACKLES OF *HUMILITY* THROWN UPON YOU.

NOW, UNTOLD *LIGHT YEARS* BETWEEN HERE AND EARTH--

"AND NOTHING CHANGES."

"THEY DOMINATE US WITH NOTHING BUT PIECES OF PAPER SAYING THAT THEY ARE IN CHARGE."

"THESE MEN. THESE WEAK MEN THAT NEVER FOUGHT FOR ANYTHING."

"THEY PLEASURE THEMSELVES TO OUR SUBMISSION.

"RULES AND REGULATIONS. LAW AND ORDER--

"ALL MANIPULATIONS CREATED TO KEEP THE BOOT OF THE WEAK ON THE NECK OF THE STRONG.

PILOTS, RETURN TO A DISTANCE OF NO MORE THAN *EIGHTY KILOMETERS!*

DON'T LET THEM LEAD YOU AWAY FROM THE SHIP! *PROTECT THE SHIP!*

"ALLOWING HEROES TO DIE, SO THAT COWARDS MAY LIVE.

"YES, TODAY WE'LL FOLLOW ORDERS.

"WE WILL BE GOOD BOYS."

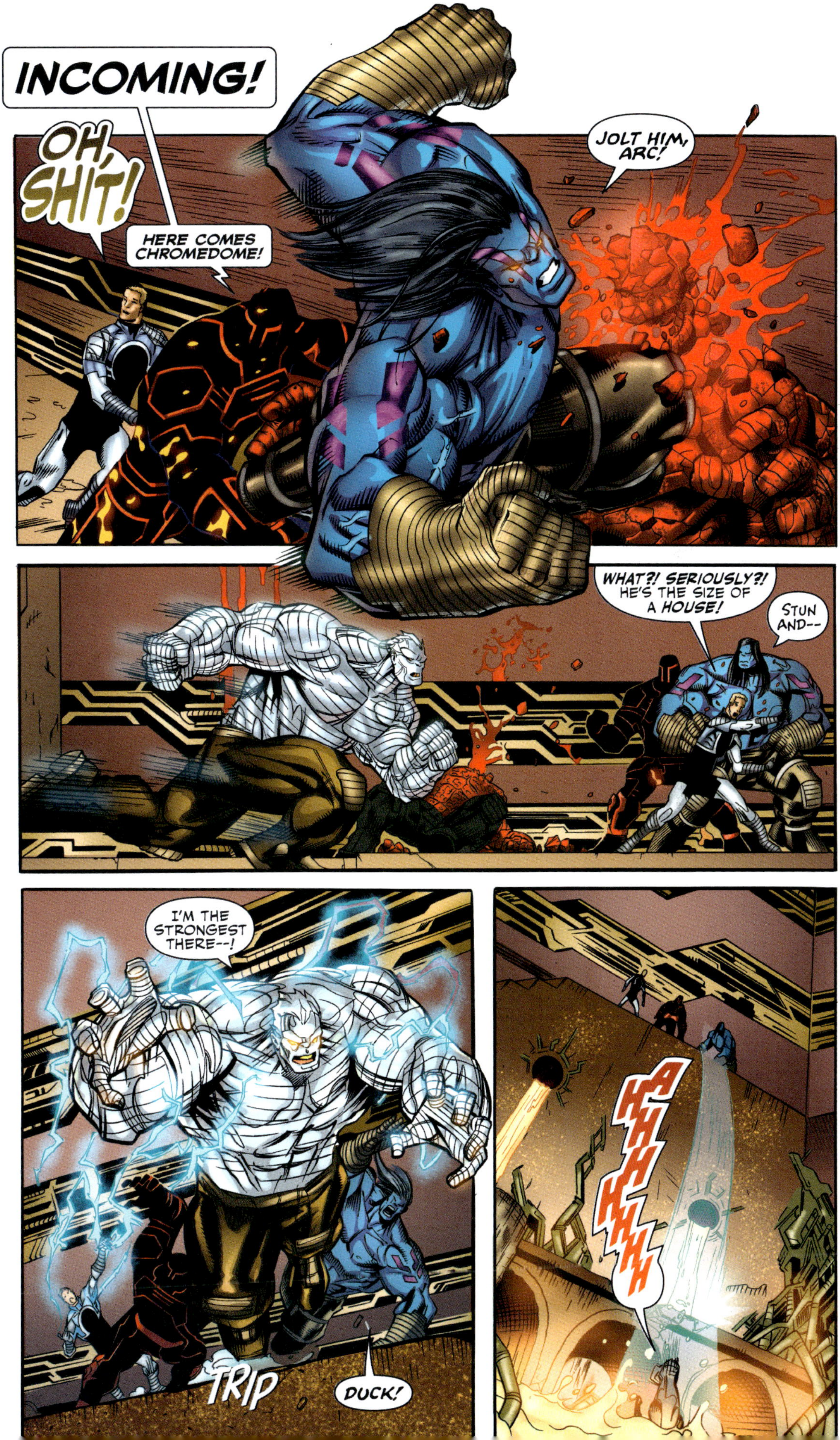

GO!

HE'S AT THE LEDGE, HI-FI!

TAKE OUT HIS LEGS!

OKAY!

BOOM!

BOOM!

BOOM! BOOM!

THREE DOWN. TWO TO GO!

YOU KIDS WILL NEVER--

GAAAHHH!

CRONOS, LOOK ALIVE!

AWWW, MAN!

I'M ALMOST LOCKED IN BY A SIZE TEN THOUSAND!

GOTTA ROLL!

BOOYAH! AND--AND-- DON'T TREAD ON ME, BRUH!

PERFECT TIME FOR THAT.

CRONOS! YOU'RE ALIVE!

HE'S NOT THE ONLY ONE, BOY!

EPILOGUE

LOCKED

UNLOCKED

GEORGY PORGY RAN AWAY.

Dedicated to Gail Simone.

THINGS TO COME...